# DEATH AT THE ICE HOTEL
WANDERLUST MYSTERIES
BOOK ONE

ANGIE FOX
KC BAILEY

# ALSO BY ANGIE FOX

**THE SOUTHERN GHOST HUNTER SERIES**

Southern Spirits

A Ghostly Gift (short story)

The Skeleton in the Closet

Ghost of a Chance (short story)

The Haunted Heist

Deader Homes & Gardens

Dog Gone Ghost (short story)

Sweet Tea and Spirits

Murder on the Sugarland Express

Pecan Pies and Dead Guys

The Mint Julep Murders

The Ghost of Christmas Past

Southern Bred and Dead

The Haunted Homecoming

Give Up the Ghost

Dread and Buried

Death at the Drive-In

Secrets, Lies and Fireflies

**THE MONSTER MASH TRILOGY**

The Monster MASH

The Transylvania Twist

Werewolves of London

**THE ACCIDENTAL DEMON SLAYER SERIES**

The Accidental Demon Slayer

The Dangerous Book for Demon Slayers

A Tale of Two Demon Slayers

The Last of the Demon Slayers

My Big Fat Demon Slayer Wedding

Beverly Hills Demon Slayer

Night of the Living Demon Slayer

What To Expect When Your Demon Slayer is Expecting

**SHORT STORY COLLECTIONS:**

Haunted for Christmas: A collection of Southern Ghost Hunter short stories

A Little Night Magic: A collection of Southern Ghost Hunter and Accidental Demon Slayer short stories

# ALSO BY KC BAILEY

Writing as Kristin Bailey for teen readers

Legacy of the Clockwork Key

Rise of the Arcane Fire

Shadow of the War Machine

The Silver Gate

Into the Nightfell Wood

WANDERLUST BOOK ONE

# Death at the Ice Hotel

*NEW YORK TIMES* BESTSELLING AUTHOR
## ANGIE FOX & KC BAILEY

Copyright © 2025 by Angie Fox

Copyright © 2025 by KC Bailey

All rights reserved.

No part of this book may be reproduced in any form or by any electronic or mechanical means, including information storage and retrieval systems, without written permission from the author, except for the use of brief quotations in a book review.

DEATH AT THE ICE HOTEL

ISBN: 979-8-9921819-2-0

*To Aileen, who's been feeding my tacky earring addiction and reading my stories since shoulder pads were in style. The fashion choices have been questionable, but the friendship is perfect.*
*This one's for you.*
*—Angie Fox*

*This book is dedicated to the cherished memory of Aunt Lois. You were a fan from the very beginning, and your support meant the world to me. You would have loved this one. We all miss you.*
*—KC Bailey*

## CHAPTER ONE

"We have to protect the rebel base!" Leia slapped her waterproof gloves against the snowy wall. If she could pack it solid enough, even Darth Vader wouldn't be able to find them here on Hoth.

Her best friends, Jen and Kat, piled heaps of snow on the walls as heavy flakes drifted down from the dark gray sky. They clung to Jen's braids as she popped up on the other side.

"We played *Empire Strikes Back* yesterday." Jen dumped a new load of snow on top of the wall, sending it tumbling over the edge straight onto Leia's head.

She was about to get buried like a dead tauntaun.

"Look at this snow." Leia scooped a bunch up in her arms and tried to hug it onto the wall. "We have to play Hoth." Maybe her body heat would melt it into ice, and it would be stronger that way. "The fort can't withstand more than a hundred stormtroopers at this rate. It doesn't even have a roof."

"I can make a roof." Jen launched herself over the wall,

nearly knocking it down. "I'm the fairy ice queen. I'll use my magic." She twirled like a ballerina.

"Faster," Leia urged. "It's working! We'll have a rebel base in no time."

Kat popped around the corner, wielding one Barbie dressed warmly in Leia's mom's fur-cuffed slipper, and another one in a swimsuit. "Good. Because Arctic Explorer Barbie has almost found the South Pole, but a storm is blowing in. She needs to get out of the blizzard."

"She can stay here." Leia packed another handful of snow into place. "Soon, we'll have a landing pad big enough for a star cruiser."

"The roof is almost finished." Jen retrieved the blanket Leia's mom had given them to keep their knees dry, tossing it over the top of the fort before piling on snow. "It's beautiful!" The words had barely left her mouth when the whole base collapsed on top of them.

Thwump!

Jen and Kat squealed.

Leia pushed through the chunks of snow, swimming in the ruins of the Hoth base. "Oh no. The *Millenium Falcon* is buried. We'll never escape!"

"Avalanche Rescue Barbie is on the way!" Kat's voice emerged from somewhere in the snow pile.

"And the fairy ice queen ruled them all," Jen declared, popping up like a womp rat from its burrow.

Leia's mom stood over them. When had she gotten there?

"Okay, you three. All rebels, fairy queens, and Rescue Barbies need to fall back to the kitchen base."

"We're *busy*." Leia slumped in the snow.

"You've been out all day. I made Rice Krispie treats and cocoa."

# CHAPTER ONE

Kat's hand shot up through the snow. "Yes!" All three of them scrambled to their feet and raced to the house.

A few minutes later, Leia cradled a mug of cocoa in her stinging hands. Steam curled up from the marshmallows while Kat and Jen bounced in their chairs around the kitchen table, leaving puddles of melted snow beneath their seats.

"This one's a whopper. It's coming straight off the lake." Leia's mom spoke into the phone as their yellow-naped amazon parrot, Charley, paced back and forth on the counter. He spread his wings like a territorial goose, taking aim at the phone cord with his beak until her mom scooped him up and plunked him back on his perch. "Don't risk it. I can keep the girls here for the night." Leia sat up straighter at that. "Take care. We'll dig out in the morning."

Kat's mug tipped precariously as she shot up in her chair. "Sleepover? Eeeeeeeeeeeee!"

"That means we get to spend the night in the ice fort," Leia declared as Charley abandoned his perch to land on her head. She snuck him a piece of Rice Krispie treat before Mom scooped the bird up again. Charley squawked in protest.

"I'm sorry, sweetie, but the rebel base is in rubble, and the sun is setting on Hoth." Mom handed Charley a slice of apple and whisked the bird into the other room to return him to his cage.

"Shoot." Leia planted her elbows on the table. "Maybe if we asked again, real nice."

"It is a tough place to spend the night." Kat licked marshmallow from her fingers before reaching for a second Rice Krispie treat. "I've seen plenty of arctic explorers end up like human popsicles. Even Luke Skywalker barely made it, and he needed a tauntaun sleeping bag."

True. "But I still wish we could do it."

Jen's eyes sparked with that special gleam that always meant trouble—or magic. Usually both. She planted her elbows on the table and rested her chin in her palms. "I know how to make a wish come true."

"How?" Kat asked through a mouthful of Krispie treat.

"Fairy magic."

"Of course." Kat exchanged a knowing look with Leia. "I think she might really be part fairy."

Leia didn't doubt it.

Jen darted from the room, her sock feet sliding on the linoleum. She returned clutching Leia's My Little Pony lunchbox, paper, and the glitter pens she'd given Leia for her birthday.

"It's simple, really." She uncapped an emerald-green pen that sparkled like fairy dust. "All you have to do is write down your wish, and then we'll wish as hard as we can together."

"Yes!" Leia grabbed a slip of paper, her hand shaking with excitement as she wrote *I wish we could spend the night in the snow fort.*

"Please, please, please, please, please," she chanted with each letter before passing the paper to Jen.

"Now for the fairy magic." Jen's fingers moved with practiced precision, creasing once, twice, folding it into a perfect origami heart. "There." She held it up like a precious gem. "Now kiss it for extra wish power, and we'll put it in the box."

"You think it'll work?" Leia asked as the lonely paper heart fell into the plastic case.

"I know it will," Jen said, closing the lid and placing her hand on top. Leia added hers immediately.

Kat's hand topped the stack. "If we all wish hard enough."

❋

FORTY YEARS LATER, Leia hunched over her kitchen counter, carefully positioning the last piece of her mosaic backsplash. She'd been replacing the decades-old tile, one scraped-out section at a time, with bits of broken plates and pottery, creating a tropical forest scene with birds, inspired by her favorite bird, Charley.

Her coffee sat forgotten nearby as she squinted, trying to find the perfect spot for a fragment of her grandmother's favorite teacup.

The chicken soup she'd set out to cool balanced precariously near her elbow. She'd planted it within arm's reach, knowing better than to leave it unguarded. Charley was her joy and her love, but her bird was also a notorious noodle thief.

"Bing-bong!" Charley announced from the perch near the front window.

"I'm not falling for it this time." Leia reached for her coffee without looking up. "The last time you sent me to the door, you flew in here and stole the cheese off my sandwich. I was stuck with ham and nothing."

Charley let out a little, "Heh-heh-heh," sounding suspiciously like a supervillain, then squawked, "Bing-bong!"

The aroma of herbs and broth filled the kitchen, making her stomach growl. She'd rather not come back to find no noodles.

*Ding-dong!* The bell rang for real.

Charley danced back and forth across the perch, looking far too pleased.

"I think I owe you an apology," Leia said, sparing a pat on the head for Charley as she headed for the door. "And maybe a noodle."

"Treat!" Charley squawked triumphantly, landing on Leia's shoulder as she opened the door.

A mysterious package sat on the porch, definitely not something she'd ordered.

*Weird.*

"Weird!" Charley echoed. "Whatcha doin', wierdo bird? That's weird!"

She hadn't realized she'd said it out loud.

The simple cardboard box bore only her name and address on a typed mail sticker.

No return address.

She carried it into the kitchen and sliced it open.

No doubt her mom was at it again. She'd been decluttering like a madwoman. The last time her parents had come through town in their RV, they'd dropped off her pink Huffy bike and her entire wardrobe from high school—when she'd been a size four. She'd told them not to bother, to just donate it all to someone who could use it.

But...

She dug through a mound of crumpled-up newspaper and gasped.

She was so glad they didn't listen. Her hands trembled slightly as she lifted her My Little Pony lunch box out of the wrapping. The pudgy old-school ponies pranced on a green hill with daisies, unaware of how gloriously round they looked.

*The wish box.*

"Ooo..." Charley leaned in for a closer look, nearly toppling off her shoulder.

"Do you remember this?" She pushed back the clips and

slowly lifted the lid. "I do." Dozens upon dozens of neatly folded paper hearts filled the box to the brim.

Each one held a memory, a dream, a moment of magic she and her best friends had created together.

She picked a wish from the top and unfolded it, smiling at the childish handwriting, which hadn't faded in forty years.

She turned to her bird. "I'm going to do something wild, Charley." She reached into her back pocket for her phone.

"Brrrrrrrrrrrrrring!" Charley exclaimed as she dialed, in a remarkable impression of the old phone that hung on the wall in the kitchen in Grand Rapids.

"That's right, Charley, brrrring."

"Hey, DIY queen," Kat answered over the beep of hospital monitors and the barely contained chaos behind the nurses' station. "How's Charley?"

"On the way to nab a noodle," Leia answered as Charley waddled toward the kitchen.

"That bird still owes me a piece of pizza from the last time I visited."

"You were the one who tried to answer the door at midnight." At least Leia had an excuse to be distracted. "Listen. I have a crazy idea."

## CHAPTER
# TWO

Leia scanned the flood of travelers pouring through the airport arrival gate, her heart quickening as she searched for the only face in the crowd that mattered.

But it was the earrings she recognized first.

Dangling from the lobes of an otherwise sensible-looking woman with short salt-and-pepper curls were the two gaudiest red parrots in coconut trees that money could buy. The sight made Leia's chest tighten with affection.

Leia had chosen to wear an equally embarrassing set from her own vast collection of tacky earrings—a pair of fortune cookies dangling from little Chinese takeout boxes. It had become a bit of a running joke between the two of them.

One that showed no signs of slowing down.

"Aaaaaaahhhh!" Leia tried to rush forward, but it came off as more of a lurch as she staggered under her heavy backpack and dragged a stuffed suitcase. "I can't believe you made it. I can't believe we're doing this. I can't believe you're wearing the earrings I sent you!"

Kat, who was clearly more sensible about packing for trips, zipped to Leia and enveloped her in a hug. "I can't believe my flight out of Baltimore was this late. Time to book it, or we're going to miss the plane to Duluth."

"Right, right," Leia said, "but I can't help it." She hugged Kat again. "It's been too long since I've seen you."

"Long enough to dye your hair," Kat teased. "I love the rebel look."

"If you're going to cover your grays, you might as well cover them with something interesting."

"True." Kat adjusted the shoulder strap on her bag, then paled when she saw the Departures screen. "We have to cross terminals. We're never going to make it."

"We've got this." Sure, it would be tight, but Leia had faith, and they had no other choice. "Come on. Remember that time we almost missed our flight to Cancun?"

She zigzagged through the crowd, her overstuffed roller bag threatening rebellion with each swerve. Kat's practical carry-on glided smoothly as she matched Leia's pace.

"The gate agent opened the door for us because you told her we were bridesmaids." Kat's half laugh, half groan echoed through the terminal.

"You were my bridesmaid." Leia wrestled her suitcase around a corner.

"Six years later," Kat panted, maintaining her white-knuckle grip on her shoulder bag.

Their window of opportunity was closing fast. Leia put on a burst of speed.

Together they raced past restaurants and shops and strollers and Starbucks lines. Leia's calves burned. It had been years since she'd been in an airport, and maybe it had been a mistake to wait to meet Kat at her gate, but she couldn't imagine getting on the plane without her. It had

# CHAPTER TWO

also been years since she'd run anywhere. She should have stretched first.

Where had the time gone?

Her phone buzzed, and a familiar green-feathered face filled the screen.

"Seriously, Charley?" She jabbed the decline button.

Kat's breathless laugh carried forward. "Your bird is calling you?"

"Nick must have given her the iPad again." Leia shook her head, remembering how a simple research project about anxious parrots and video chatting had created a technological monster.

Next thing Leia knew, Nick had rigged up an iPad for Charley, complete with custom icons for her favorite humans.

"Charley isn't going to like that you ghosted her." Just then Kat's phone trilled, and Charley's face popped up on her screen.

To Leia's shock, Kat answered.

Charley's feathered face took up the entire video-chat screen, one blazing orange eye coming in for a closeup. "Hiiiiiiiiiii!" Charley's parroty voice cut above the din of the terminal. "Whatcha doin, Charley? Hiiiiiiii."

"My bird is calling you?" Leia stumbled, losing her grip on her bag, cringing as it spun sideways. Frickity frick!

Kat seized the handle of Leia's rebellious roller bag, steadying it. "Hi, pretty bird. Thanks for calling. I can't talk, okay? I gotta run."

"Wheeeeeeeee!" Charley squawked as Kat ended the call.

"She's a smart girl, and I don't want to discourage her," Kat explained.

*Smarter than us*, Leia thought. Her family had thought

Charley was a boy for the first three years. Then she'd laid an egg.

Kat gave Leia a thump on the back. "Come on. If we miss this flight, we're screwed. You're the one who used to run track."

"I haven't run this much in thirty years." Leia threw herself forward anyway. "And I'm wearing snow boots." But they'd both put down a lot of money for this trip, and this was the only flight to Duluth. She did not want to spend the night in a hotel next to O'Hare with a scenic view of the parking lot, video-chatting with her pet parrot.

Together they raced to the gate, arriving at the empty bay of chairs just as the airline attendant reached for the PA system.

*Last call for flight 544 to Duluth.*

They'd made it!

Leah was thrilled. Elated. And a little shocked. Kat beamed as she scanned her boarding pass while Leia struggled to swipe away Charley's missed call and pull up her ticket.

The blast of cold air from the jet bridge had never felt so good.

"We've still got it." Kat held her chin high as they sideshuffled down the narrow aisle toward their seats. "And we don't have to pretend we're packing pink taffeta bridesmaids dresses."

"Or that we're running the Boston marathon tomorrow."

"On our way to Duluth." Kat laughed, her eyes crinkling with the same mischief they'd held since grade school.

"I doubt any of it would work these days." They struggled to find a place for Leia's bulging luggage before the flight attendant gave up on them and insisted she gate-check it. Kat's sensible carry-on slid perfectly under the seat while Leia resorted to kicking her backpack into submission with one snow boot.

She gripped the armrests as the engines roared to life and sent them sailing into the sky.

When her heart slowed again, Leia smiled at her old friend, so very glad to be in an uncomfortable seat, packed into coach, flying north into the Minnesota wilderness in January.

Kat fiddled with her disco Snoopy watchband. "Jen would be glad we're doing this. And she would have adored your hair."

Leia ran a hand through her chin-grazing cut. In a pique of middle-age rebellion, she'd dyed it bright pink. It had faded, and quite possibly made her resemble the ponies on the lunch box, but she didn't care. It was a small act of defiance against the march of time. "I can't believe it's been four years since the funeral. Every so often the phone rings, and I still think it's her."

"Me too," Kat admitted. "But most of the time, it's your bird."

Leia snorted. "This is crazy. I still can't believe we pulled this trip together in less than a week."

"Please." Kat grinned. "I can be packed and on a plane to anywhere in less than an hour. Crisis-response nursing teaches you how to travel light."

Leia knew all about Kat's go-pack. Whenever an earthquake, hurricane, or other emergency struck, Kat would be there. "With three changes of clothes, six phone chargers, and your lucky rubber duck."

She had a whole collection, named after famous nurses.

Kat perked up. "I brought Florence Waddlegale this time."

Of course she did. "I still don't know how you do it, Kat—dropping into crisis zones with barely more than a toothbrush."

"It's part of the job." She shrugged. "And it's Katherine now, remember?"

"Right. You say that"—Leia tilted her head—"but I'm sorry. You're Kat to me. This dog is too old to learn a new trick."

"Well, then you're the rebel princess who gets a special exception." Kat closed her eyes. "I'd love to see the wish box again."

"I brought it," Leia said, reaching down to unzip her backpack.

"Of course you did," Kat said. "So how many wishes are in there?"

"Take a look," Leia said, retrieving the box. "We must have added at least three wishes at every slumber party since we were seven."

"Until we discovered boys."

"And makeup."

"And malls."

Kat's eyes twinkled as Leia cracked open the box.

Inside, the origami hearts nestled together, each one a childhood wish folded up tight. A wave of memories hit her—late-night giggles, pinky swears, and big plans whispered in the dark.

The first wish remained open on top of the others.

*I wish we could spend the night in the snow fort.*

"Leave it to you to make your wish come true," Kat said.

"Hey, we've been waiting forty years for a snow roof." When she'd seen the message, she remembered an article about the Northern Magic Ice Festival. It featured an ice-sculpting competition and an ice hotel they built every year at a remote lakeside resort in Minnesota.

It was perfect.

It was also last minute, and the only experience she could book was a high-priced weekend in a private cabin for the festival, with an exclusive room for one night in the ice hotel designed by one of the ice-sculpting competitors.

The whole thing was overwhelming. And exciting. And did she mention overwhelming? But she worked hard, and she'd earned a crazy girls' weekend. At least that was what her husband had said when she'd told him about her idea.

And so began the adventure that led them to meet up at O'Hare and make the mad dash for the flight to Duluth. To the here and now.

"An ice hotel is a glorified snow fort," Leia insisted.

"Absolutely," Kat said without missing a beat. "So what else is in here?" She poked a finger among the hearts.

"I haven't opened them, and I don't think we should. Not yet. Unless we're going on more trips."

"So wait." Kat paused, her expression shifting to that familiar look of careful consideration. "Are you saying you want to do the entire lunchbox full?"

"Gosh, no. I only intended to do the one. This is a wild lark, remember?"

"There was a time you would have attempted anything in that box," Kat said.

They both would have.

"Let's see how this weekend goes," Leia hedged.

She hadn't let herself travel much lately. First, it had been one job, then the next, and the next. Then it had been marriage and raising kids, and then Charley came to live with her because Mom's arthritis was getting bad. Now?

Well, her home had become her castle, her safe harbor in a chaotic world.

While Kat jetted off to disaster zones, Leia had mastered the art of staying put.

What she hadn't realized until she planned their spontaneous weekend was that she'd gotten out of the habit of doing anything frivolous. Like trekking out to an ice hotel to relive a childhood fantasy with a girlfriend who knew her better than she knew herself.

They exchanged a conspiratorial look. How did Kat manage to make her feel like no time at all had passed?

"Okay," Kat said, straightening her shoulders. "Let's live our ice-hotel fantasy this weekend. Then if we decide we want to, we'll pick another wish out of the box. But if we open it, we have to do it. Deal?" Kat held out her hand with her pinky finger crooked.

The gesture hit Leia with unexpected force. How many promises had they sealed this way?

Leia tilted her head. "You realize we put some bizarre things in there. At least I know I did."

Kat shot her a playful smirk. "I think I did too."

Leia hooked her pinky with her old friend's. "Then let's see what happens. Count me in."

## CHAPTER
# THREE

Katherine felt like a rebel. And she didn't regret it a bit. Her heart soared as she took in the elegant timber framing of the rustic resort.

Tall pines surrounded the lodge, dusted with sugar-like snow.

"It's amazing." Leia hugged herself against the cold as she climbed out of the cab. The wind picked up and sent icy crystals swirling in the air. "Whew, let's get inside."

Leia led the charge through the rough-hewn wooden doors into the lobby. The warm air greeted them with a powerful whoosh, carrying the rich aroma of cinnamon and cedar.

A fresh-faced young woman at the front desk smiled at them. "Hello, and welcome to the Jack Oak Resort. How can I help you?"

While Leia handled check-in, Katherine surveyed the lobby. A waterfall tumbled over granite boulders near the elevators. Antler chandeliers decked in sparkling white holiday lights cast a shimmering lattice across the room. Pine garlands wove through the wooden rafters and draped from the banisters. The grand stone fireplace crackled, inviting guests to linger on plush leather sofas.

*I needed this*, Katherine realized. After countless nights in disaster zones and cheap hotels, it was about time she treated herself.

"Get out of town." Leia's sharp inhale brought her back to the moment. Leia chewed her lip—which was not a good sign—as she perused a piece of paper. The hostess offered her a pen to sign. "Kat, you have to see this."

Katherine scanned the list of room-damage penalties, her medical brain automatically calculating the cost-to-injury ratios. She whistled, her eyebrows climbing at the very real, very scary financial penalties for anything that they damaged in the ice hotel. "Rumpelstiltskin demanded less."

"Whatever you do, don't touch the walls," Leia warned.

"Or have a biological event in the sleeping bags," Katherine said as she signed with a flourish. "Pressure's on. We'd better behave."

Leia tapped a finger on the counter as she took up the pen. "This is us, remember?"

Things tended to go a little sideways when they got together, but they hadn't been arrested. So far, anyway.

"I'll keep you in line," Katherine vowed.

"I can't say the same for you." Leia put the pen to paper and signed.

It was done.

The desk clerk handed them each an information packet. "The grand opening for the ice hotel is tonight in the ice bar. Keep these VIP passes attached to your coats. Here are the keys to cabin two." She produced a map and circled a small square. "Follow this path to the right, and you'll find it in the group of cabins closest to the lakeshore. Leave your luggage here. We'll deliver it shortly."

Their cabin was nestled in a small cluster with two other cabins that shared a firepit, hot tub and sauna. Three more cabin trios dotted the landscape, one to the north of theirs and two on the eastern side of the large central plaza. The ice hotel stood at the center, a striking focal point between the lodge and the frozen lake.

"For your night in the ice hotel itself, you will be in room nineteen on Saturday," the hostess continued, circling it. "And if you'd like to watch the artists working on their sculptures for the competition, that's happening right here on the lakeshore. Did you watch the video about your stay in the ice hotel?"

Video? Leia glanced at her. "There was a video?"

The woman at the desk smiled as if she'd heard it all before. "The link was in your confirmation email."

Katherine shrugged. "We'll play it by ear." Like any last-minute adventure.

Leia looked at her like she'd sprouted an extra head. "We'll watch the video," she said to the desk clerk.

Their hostess reached under the desk. "Here, take this fact sheet. It has helpful tips and lists the web page with the link."

Leia eased her overstuffed backpack off her shoulders, nearly toppling her front-heavy roller bag. "I have arctic-rated boots, thermal socks, fleece underwear, five different kinds of lip balm, a full ski suit, a gourmet hot chocolate kit, and hand warmers by the dozen, but I somehow missed the video?"

"Don't be so hard on yourself." Katherine set her single bag alongside Leia's tank of a suitcase. "And did you say hot chocolate?" She was in the habit of packing light, but there was something to be said for bringing your own chocolate to the party.

"I've missed you." Leia's voice softened as they pushed through tall arched doors opposite the main entrance.

A rush of heated air bid them farewell as they stepped into the glorious Minnesota winter. The cold hit Katherine's face like a familiar friend, so different from the sweltering heat of her latest assignment in Bogotá.

"I've missed you, too." Katherine breathed in the crystal-clear air. "And this." Just being together. Without a care in the world.

Snow crunched beneath their boots as they followed the path, their breath creating delicate clouds in the crisp air. Katherine took a moment to admire the beauty surrounding her, the trees, the snow, the air itself, and the way colors shifted over the windswept ice.

Leia kept craning her neck toward the open plaza. Katherine caught glimpses of large white mounds peeking between the evergreens lining the path.

"You're not even looking," Leia said.

"Not yet."

Leia was never one to hold back her curiosity, but Katherine could wait a bit to see what the ice hotel had in store. The woods and wilderness held enough wonder for her.

Soon, their little cluster of cabins came into view.

"Which one is ours?" Leia craned her neck, picking up the pace.

"This one." Cabin two. Right in the middle.

"You always did have a better sense of direction than me," Leia said as she doubled back. "Did you know that people who live in grid-pattern cities are actually worse at

## CHAPTER THREE

navigation than those who grow up in cities with a mishmash of streets? It's all about spatial awareness."

"I don't live anywhere," Katherine joked. It wasn't strictly true. She maintained an apartment in Baltimore near the University Medical Center, but she was hardly ever there.

Katherine's boots created a resonant thump as she mounted the porch steps. The quaint cabin was the picture of cozy living, its wooden logs and stone foundation frosted with snow and framed by tall pines. The firepit anchored a friendly circle of benches at the center of their cabin cluster. Nearby, a hot tub and sauna sat idle, promising warmth against the chilly air.

She swiped the key card and pushed the door open, stepping into the embrace of the log cabin.

The living area welcomed them first. A plush sofa faced a gas fireplace in the corner. Vintage ski posters added splashes of color—reds and blues that popped against the wood-paneled walls. A pair of antique snowshoes, crossed in an X, celebrated the spirit of winter adventure.

Leia bounced into the kitchenette, running her hand over a gleaming black countertop. "I think I want to live here."

Katherine checked out the coffee selection. "This beats a tent in Bogotá, where the local roosters thought three a.m. was sunrise."

Open shelves displayed an array of ceramic dishes and mugs waiting to be filled. A small stove, its kettle perched atop, promised the comfort of a hot drink, and a half-sized refrigerator hummed softly.

Beyond the living area, a pair of bedroom doors stood ajar, revealing quilt-topped beds and the soft glow of lamplight.

This was more than Katherine had anticipated when Leia had called her out of the blue with her "crazy idea." The wooden floors creaked gently underfoot, and the windows, framed with plaid curtains, revealed a scene that would make Bob Ross weep with joy.

"Take a look at this." Leia stood at a rough-hewn coffee table, bent over a large photo book. Its cover bore the image of an intricate ice castle. Inside, the high-resolution photographs captured the stark beauty of transient masterpieces carved with painstaking detail by competitors from around the world.

"Now that's talent." Leia turned to a glossy page showing a sculpture of eagles in flight, soaring at least twenty feet over the team who had created it. Their tails became a flow of water with leaping salmon and hulking bears catching the fish in a tumbling current of glowing ice. The lead artist stood next to it in a crimson stocking cap, sporting a lopsided smile while his team knelt solemnly in front.

"I can't believe that one came in second," Katherine said, reading the caption. She'd never seen anything like it, certainly not on that scale.

But that display was the tip of the proverbial iceberg.

Between stunning masterpieces were candid photos of the sculpting teams on scaffolding, wielding blowtorches, or having impromptu water-gun fights. The close-knit camaraderie reminded Katherine of a tribe of night-shift nurses. The kind who had each other's backs.

"Here's the winner," Leia said, running a finger over the opposing page. An ice ballerina, frozen mid-arabesque, danced among a troupe of graceful swans.

The sculpture was a marvel of craftsmanship and fluidity. Her limbs extended in long gravity-defying lines, her skirt seemingly caught mid-flutter. The artist had mastered the illusion of texture, suggesting delicate lace along the hem of her tutu and soft fabric wrapped around her bun.

Katherine leaned closer. "Look at her face—the muscle definition is incredible. She almost looks like she's breathing."

The final page showed a young woman with windswept hair done up in a careless braid beneath a wool hat. Sporty sunglasses shielded her eyes as she laughed, holding a chainsaw aloft over massive ice blocks stacked on the frozen ground, her boot sunk deep in the snow behind her.

*In memory of Rebecca Hardney. Fierce competitor, cherished friend.*

Katherine's heart clenched. Dang. The woman had been younger than Jen when she passed. After twenty-odd years in emergency medicine, death shouldn't surprise her anymore, but it always did.

Leia studied Rebecca's face. "What do you think happened to her?"

"There's no telling." Katherine's voice held the careful neutrality she used with worried families in the ER. She flipped the photobook over, embossed letters catching the light. *Created by Amy Wu.*

A rattle at the door broke the moment. "That's probably our luggage," Katherine said, heading over.

"Wouldn't they just knock?"

"Unless this is the part where we find out we've accidentally joined a cabin timeshare presentation."

"In that case, we can reenact Operation Sneak Out to See Bon Jovi." Leia's eyes sparkled with mischief.

They'd been sophomores in high school, and she still couldn't believe that they hadn't been caught.

Katherine opened the door to find a surprised woman

in a hot pink ski jacket fumbling with a key card in her bulky gloves. "Oh! Excuse me!" Her eyes widened as she pushed a pink paisley headband back over neat rows of her silver woven braids.

"Trishelle!" A man's voice echoed from the path near the hot tub. He was as sturdy as the pines and brandished a neon green pool noodle. "We're in number three. That's number two!"

Trishelle took a quick step back, her fingers flying to her mouth. "I am so sorry. I am definitely at the wrong door."

"No worries," Katherine said. "First time here?"

"Oh no." She smiled warmly. "We've been coming up for the competition every year since it started. Mostly with my best friend and her husband. I apologize. I must have been on autopilot. Rita and Tony always stayed in this cabin, and I guess my feet just found the way."

Her husband waved the pool noodle at her like a lighthouse beacon. "Love, Rita and Tony haven't come to the festival in four years."

"You hush." Trishelle snatched the noodle and bopped him on the head with it. "Feet have a long memory."

Leia leaned over the porch rail. "I've never seen hot tub pool toys."

"Neither have I." Trishelle hefted the noodle. "This here is our boot rack."

MacGyver could eat his heart out. These two clearly had things covered.

"I'm John," her husband offered. "Trishelle was just rushing to get down to the shore and see how the sculptures are shaping up."

"I'm Katherine, and this is my friend Leia."

Leia extended her hand over the rail. "Looks like we're

neighbors for the weekend. Sorry we're not your old friends."

Trishelle's smile was so warm it could've melted the ice sculptures. "Well, that doesn't mean we can't become new ones."

"Luggage incoming," John announced, shielding his eyes.

A compact figure in black approached on an ATV with a custom luggage rack welded on the back.

"Ian!" John's welcome echoed across the snow. "How did the hotel shape up this year?"

"She's a beauty." The spritely hotel worker enveloped John and Trishelle in a bear hug before gracefully transferring Leia's suitcase to the porch. "Welcome to the Jack Oak." He retrieved their remaining bags with the agility of a tundra rabbit.

"Ian, meet Katherine and Leia." John gestured. "Ian is the jack-of-all-trades around here."

"Glad you came to visit the land of ice and...more ice," Ian quipped, depositing John's and Trishelle's bags. "Enjoy your stay. And remember if you see a snowman moving suspiciously fast, it's probably just me on my rounds." With a wave, he revved up the ATV and glided away.

"Hey," John said, "we're heading down to the lake as soon as we get the luggage inside. Want to join?"

"Yes!" Trishelle perked up. "We can show you around and introduce you to the teams. I've missed having someone to hang around the competition with. Today is the most exciting day."

Katherine exchanged a quick glance with Leia. "Sold. Meet you by the sauna in five?"

"Perfect!" Trishelle retreated to their cabin to help John.

"What makes today so exciting?" Leia called after them.

Trishelle turned, walking backward with surprising grace. "They're doing precision stacking. The entire sculpture can break if they're not smart, fast, and dead-on accurate."

John sobered. "It's the most dangerous part."

"One wrong cut and..." Trishelle trailed off as if unwilling to finish.

John said it for her. "Someone could get killed."

## CHAPTER
# FOUR

Leia's breath puffed in little clouds as she trotted down the path, her heavy boots crunching through the snow. The vast expanse of the frozen lake gleamed like a mirror, forcing her to squint despite her reflective sunglasses.

She quickened her pace to catch up with Trishelle and John. Their vibrant jackets stood out against the white landscape like exotic birds in a snowy forest. And frankly, exotic birds were kinda her thing.

"I'm so excited to be here," Leia said, falling into step beside them. "I've never seen an ice sculpture in person before. The closest I've come is the swan-shaped ice mold at my cousin's wedding, and that was barely a foot tall."

"You're in for a treat, then," Trishelle said. "Just wait until you see what these artists can do with a block of ice and a chainsaw."

John rubbed his gloved hands together. "I'm counting down the minutes until we hit the ice bar tonight."

"You mean you can't wait to sample every drink at the ice bar tonight." Trishelle poked him with her elbow.

"I'm not that sturdy." John flashed a roguish grin. "Besides, tonight's our chance to explore all the rooms. I hope we've snagged an Ice King suite."

Kat canted her head. "Ice King?"

"Is there an Ice Queen?" Leia asked.

"If so, this sounds like prom all over again," Kat deadpanned, earning a snort from Leia.

John grinned. "Roger Cullins is the Ice King. He's a local favorite who makes the trek down from Winnipeg every year. They crowned him the Ice King because he's been the undisputed champion for four years running."

"His sculptures defy the laws of physics," Trishelle said.

John gestured enthusiastically as they walked. "It's the way he manipulates the ice. Curves, spirals, lattices that look too delicate to stand. But they do. It's nothing short of a miracle."

"Personally"—Trishelle glanced over her shoulder with a conspiratorial smile—"I get a kick out of hunting for the triangles."

"Triangles?" Kat and Leia exchanged looks, their synchronized confusion making them laugh.

"It's the Ice King's signature," John said. "He hides triangles in every hotel room he designs, regardless of the theme. Sometimes they're in your face, or oftentimes they're cleverly concealed. But they're always there. It's turned into a treasure hunt for his fans."

"Now that's my kind of challenge." Leia nudged Kat. "Remember the time we tried to hide *Star Wars* references in our science fair project?"

"And we nearly got disqualified when you called our volcano the Death Star." Kat shook her head, but her smile was fond.

"It slipped through," Leia said with a wince. "I wasn't a fact-checker then."

"Well, if you like a puzzle, you'll love this." Trishelle hugged herself against a gust of wind. "It's also enigmatic and quirky, much like the artist himself. Though, interestingly, he never incorporates triangles into his competition pieces."

As they neared the lakeshore, several sculptors were hard at work on massive blocks of ice. Their chainsaws buzzed and whined as they cut deep wedges out of enormous rectangular blocks. Crystalline spray erupted from each cut, catching the sunlight and transforming into a shimmering, diamond-like mist.

Rounding a bend, Leia gasped. Six teams of sculptors worked in perfect synchronicity, their work areas dominated by colossal ice blocks. Her artist's eye tracked the geometric precision of the scaffolding embracing the larger pieces. Above, chunks of ice swayed in neon slings like frozen pendulums hoisted skyward by the mechanical arms of boom lifts.

The creative chaos reminded her of one of her favorite DIY home remodeling shows, but on an epic scale. Team members shouted instructions over the din of the chainsaws, orchestrating an elaborate ice ballet. The steaming water guns particularly fascinated her. She watched, entranced, as liquid transformed to solid with a dramatic hiss and crackle, cementing pieces together.

Kat's elbow found her ribs. "Why didn't we think of that when we were little?"

Leia barked out a laugh. "We would have been unstoppable," she agreed, envisioning how epic the battle for Hoth could have played out with an ice fortress that didn't fall on their heads every single time.

A crowd of spectators lined the path, their chatter barely audible over the mechanical symphony. Parents tugged children in plastic sleds, their small faces alight with wonder.

A half-formed sculpture caught her attention. She squinted, making out the graceful arch of a stallion's neck, its jagged mane rippling in an invisible breeze.

"Heya, Ian!" John's voice cut through her concentration.

"Hold on," Leia said as John raised a hand to his friend perched in the cab of a nearby boom lift. "Ian delivers bags *and* runs the boom lift?"

John's laugh carried over the mechanical din. "We told you he's a jack-of-all-trades. This place wouldn't function without him. He's the foreman in charge of constructing the hotel every year."

"That man has capital-S stories," Trishelle added. "With any luck, we'll catch up with him again at the bar tonight."

Ian waved before returning to the controls. With practiced ease, he guided a massive section of rough-carved ice to the top of a towering formation, his weathered face etched with intense concentration.

"*Da!* There! Right there!" a bear of a man in a heavy wool coat bellowed, his arms windmilling as the ice swung overhead, cradled in blaze-orange straps.

Trishelle leaned close. "His team has to catch it and guide it into place."

The large man's groan echoed across the snow as he braced the ice with his broad shoulder. Leia winced in sympathy when a sudden spray of water hit his face, but he remained as steady as a statue until the sculpture set. Frost crystals bloomed in his beard while he muttered a string of colorful expletives in Russian.

When the block finally settled, he eased away with exaggerated caution, hands raised as if backing away from an armed robber. Leia's heart leapt as comprehension dawned. "Oh! It's an arm! Is this the Statue of Liberty?"

Beside her, Kat tilted her head. "Well, if it is, Lady Liberty is less about welcoming the huddled masses and more about thwacking injustice over the head with her torch."

Laughter bubbled up inside Leia. Kat's sardonic sense of humor always hit her right in the funnies. "She does look a bit militant, doesn't she?"

"Hey, Alexi!" John called out. "You're going to get frostbite, my man!"

The big man's laugh thundered across the snow. "Me?" He brushed the ice from his beard, sending a shower of crystals sparkling to the ground. "That's impossible." He lumbered over in heavy boots, engulfing John's hand in a hearty shake. "I'm part polar bear."

John clapped him on the back. "More like part abominable snowman with that wild and woolly beard of yours."

Alexi stroked his beard thoughtfully. "Ah, but beneath this rugged exterior is a mind as sharp as icicle."

"Is that so?" John's eyes twinkled. "Well then, oh wise and bearded one, what's the spectacle you've conjured up for this year?"

Alexi's thick Slavic accent wrapped around them like a warm blanket as he gestured toward the half-formed statues. "Picture this—a mythic battle of epic proportions. Here we have the goddess of winter, her icy glare potent enough to freeze the bravest of souls. And facing her, the ruler of spring, poised to melt away frost with the warmth of new life."

"And leave us without a hotel," John quipped.

Everyone laughed, but Leia barely heard them. Her mind was already painting the scene Alexi described—two powerful goddesses locked in eternal combat, winter's fury against spring's promise. "That sounds absolutely breathtaking."

Alexi swelled with pride. "I am pulling out all the stops. This will be my last year, after all."

The words snapped Leia back to reality as Trishelle's face fell. "Oh no! Why?"

Alexi crossed his arms and surveyed his team with a mixture of sadness and resolve. "It's time for me to go home. My mother, she's not getting any younger, and I need to be there for her." A heavy sigh escaped him. "I've been putting off my family for too long, chasing my dreams out here on the ice." He squared his shoulders. "I will leave as soon as the competition is finished."

"We hope you win," Kat said, raising her gloved hand with crossed fingers. Leia followed suit, touched by the sculptor's dedication to both his art and family.

Alexi huffed, his grin showing through his bushy beard. "Yes, there is always hope for that." He stroked his beard thoughtfully. "But win or lose, I'll still be the most handsome abominable snowman this competition has ever seen."

As they moved on, Leia found herself smiling. There was something endearing about a man built like a tank who could speak so tenderly about his mother.

The site buzzed with activity. Trishelle paused to return a lost mitten to a harried mom wrangling two energetic boys, while John called greetings to various teams. "Over there is Amy's crew." Leia watched the team working on what looked like scaly arches. In her mind's eye, she could already see the sinuous dragon taking shape.

## CHAPTER FOUR

"I hope we get one of Amy's rooms," Trishelle mused.

"I'm still holding out for the Ice King," Kat said wistfully.

"True, his are always amazing," Trishelle conceded. "But Amy's rooms are *sexy*." She looped her arm through John's, batting her eyelashes dramatically as they approached the next team.

A sudden hand on John's shoulder made them all start. "I should have known there would be trouble," said a roguish-looking man. His eyes crinkled with amusement above high cheekbones kissed by the hint of a tan. A neat fringe of salt-and-pepper hair peeked out from under a sleek ski hat with a baseball-cap brim. The biting wind brought a healthy glow to his cheeks.

"You're calling me trouble? I'm pretty sure you invented it," John shot back. "How's the competition shaping up this year?"

The man let out a low whistle. "I've got a good feeling, Johnny. I think this is my year, finally."

Something about the man nagged at Leia's memory. She couldn't shake the feeling she'd seen him before. Maybe it was the confident set of his shoulders or the way he wore that shiny leather jacket like it was made for him.

"Well, well." Trishelle's gaze traveled from his rugged boots to his windswept hair, lingering on the leather jacket draped over his coveralls. "If it isn't Eric, our very own ice-sculpting James Dean. I must say, the leather jacket suits you."

Eric smoothed down the front of his jacket with a practiced motion. "I thought I'd channel my inner rebel this year. You know, shake things up a bit," he added with a wink. "Might just be the secret ingredient I need to carve my way to victory."

"Is this the Ice King?" Kat extended a gloved hand.

Eric's smile flickered before returning full force. "Unfortunately, no. I'm just the court jester." He grasped Kat's hand firmly. "Eric Hardney, at your service."

Leia's thoughts stuttered to a halt. Hardney. The name from the book. She bit back the question that sprang to her lips. Asking about a dead woman during introductions seemed tactless at best.

"He's a charmer," Kat murmured beside her.

"My favorite sculptor," John boasted. "And not just because he's practically family."

"It's also because of his food," Trishelle teased.

John's eyes glazed over. "Absolutely! No one grills a steak like a Texan. He's the head chef at Flambé in Dallas." He gestured toward Leia and Kat. "*These* two are first-timers." Then, turning back to Eric with obvious excitement, he said, "I've been dying to know. Did you land the expansion for your restaurant in Vegas?"

Eric's smile faltered, his mouth pressing in a tight line. "Sadly, no. Or at least the deal hasn't worked out yet." His jaw clenched in determination. "I just can't seem to win, can I?"

"Well, if you win the competition this year, I'll bet the publicity will tip things in your favor." John gave him a hearty pat on the shoulder. "As soon as a deal is in the works, you know Rita, Tony, Trishelle and I will invest in the expansion."

"We're all so proud of your success with Flambé," Trishelle added.

Eric ducked his chin a notch. "I never would have been able to open the restaurant without all of you." He captured John's hand on his shoulder and held it there for a moment.

# CHAPTER FOUR

"Thanks again for believing in me after everything that's happened."

"So what gives you an edge this year?" Kat asked, her attention flickering to the team of sculptors hard at work behind him.

"Well, the judges look for certain things," Eric said. "Design elements, theme, technical ability, and of course," he drawled, a mischievous glint in his eye, "the danger factor."

A warm flush crept up Leia's neck despite the biting cold. "John mentioned that."

"Here," Eric offered, stepping closer. His spicy aftershave tickled her nose, a heady mix of wood and cedar. "Take a look."

The binder he unzipped revealed a wrinkled schematic protected by plastic, though too late to save it completely. Water damage had caused the ink to bleed, and a brown stain marred one corner.

But the design itself took Leia's breath away. Her inner math geek immediately engaged with the precise numbering system for each block, the detailed notes about cuts, attachment points, weights, and angles. This wasn't art—this was engineering.

The design showed Icarus in his moment of doom, twisted in agony as his wings disintegrated before an overwhelming sun. The metaphor wasn't lost on her—hubris leading to destruction.

She'd seen enough of that at the newspaper, covering stories of powerful CEOs and politicians who thought themselves untouchable, until they weren't.

It was a stark reminder.

And a wicked cool design.

"You get it, don't you?" Eric's voice was soft, and when

she glanced over, she found him studying her face with unexpected intensity. "The designs have to push the envelope of physics. The closer to the edge, the better."

She understood. And she couldn't help but wonder. "Wouldn't that make them more likely to break?"

Eric's eyes hardened. "There's one thing we never forget around here. Ice breaks."

As if summoned by Eric's words, a shattering crash ripped through the air, echoing across the clearing like a thunderclap. Leia whirled toward the sound as shouts of alarm pierced the frigid air.

Blocks of ice lay scattered like bomb debris, and atop a teetering scaffolding, a man clung desperately, his slick gloves losing their grip. Kat and John sprang into action, racing toward the unfolding disaster.

Time seemed to slow as Leia watched, horror coursing through her veins. The man's grip failed. His body arced through the air, arms windmilling frantically. The sickening thud as he hit the packed snow made her stomach lurch. He crumpled on impact.

A collective gasp rippled through the onlookers, followed by a stunned silence. A chill ran down Leia's spine as Eric's words echoed in her mind. *Ice breaks.* And sometimes, so did the things built upon it.

## CHAPTER
# FIVE

Katherine's feet pounded against the snow, her mind clicking into what she called her "code blue clarity." She glanced at her watch. 3:47 p.m. Every detail mattered.

Behind her, John's voice rang out. "Let me through! I'm a doctor!"

Trishelle echoed after him, "You're a cardiologist!"

Katherine reached the scene first, rapidly assessing the situation. Two men stood frozen, staring at their friend lying crumpled on the ground. The scaffolding above them swayed with an ominous creak.

"You!" Katherine's voice cut through the chaos. She pointed at the man wearing a striped hat. "Phone the front desk. Have them send first aid. Then call 911."

The man nodded, fumbling for his phone. She focused on the victim, quickly assessing his condition. *He's conscious, alert, and moving*. All good signs. But she didn't like the way he held his forearm across his chest. Likely a fracture.

Katherine whirled to face his teammate, her voice

ringing out once more. "You!" She gestured toward the scaffolding. "Secure that death trap. Check for loose ice. One injury's enough for today."

The man snapped to attention, nodding vigorously as he headed for the scaffold.

Kneeling beside the injured man, Katherine kept her hands gentle but firm as she began her examination. "Hey there. I'm Katherine, the ER nurse who's perfected the art of finding decent coffee in every ER from here to Fiji. Can you tell me your name? Where does it hurt?"

"P-Paul," he stammered through clenched teeth. His face twisted as he shifted. "I think I broke my arm."

Katherine bit the thumb of her glove, yanking it off with her teeth. "That was quite a fall. What's your last name, Paul?"

"I—" he began. "It hurts."

Katherine's fingers found his pulse while keeping steady eye contact. Not too thready—a good sign. "I know. Any pain in your back or neck?" Her hands moved with gentle precision, steadying his head.

Paul started to shake his head, but she held him still. "Try not to move your neck until we're sure nothing's cracked back there. Wiggle your feet for me instead?"

His boots twitched in the snow. Katherine's shoulders relaxed a fraction. Spinal cord intact.

"It's my fault." Paul winced. "I didn't double-check the straps."

"Accidents happen," Katherine replied, checking his pupils. "Even Michaelangelo probably tripped over a bucket once or twice."

Paul swallowed hard. "Roger warned us. Said someone was sabotaging our equipment." His breathing quickened. "Told us never to trust the other teams."

"I don't know about that," Katherine said, maintaining her count on his pulse. "But I do know you were lucky." He could have been killed.

He brought a shaking hand to his arm. "Somebody loosened our straps on Monday, then again Tuesday morning. I fixed them both times." He let his head fall back. "Why didn't I check today?"

John arrived, slightly winded. He noted Paul's pale face and labored breathing and immediately lifted Paul's legs onto his knee. "Possible hypovolemic shock," he muttered, meeting Katherine's eyes with a look of shared understanding.

Katherine nodded, her mind still tracking vitals. Pulse one hundred, respirations twenty-two, skin pale but warm. She gathered Paul's information—full name, age, medications, allergies, weaving each question between fragments of conversation about ice-sculpting techniques to keep him engaged.

The resort's first aid truck arrived with a reassuring rumble. Katherine and John worked in sync with the team, transferring Paul onto the backboard, then onto the four-wheeler.

As the truck pulled away, Katherine turned to find Leia crouched by the fallen scaffolding. She was examining the neon green straps where they connected the crumpled metal to a large boulder of ice. Leia scooted over to fiddle with the latch on an orange one, her expression unnervingly similar to the one she wore when she found a mistake.

Leia glanced up. "Will he be okay?"

Katherine crouched beside her friend. "I think so." She knew better than to promise. "Likely a broken arm, but his vitals were stable, and he was alert and responsive. That's a good sign." She gestured toward the strap Leia was inspecting. "What caught your attention?"

"These connecting points." Leia sat back on her heels. "This one's spring is damaged. It was bound to break."

Katherine nodded sharply. A preventable injury. That made it even worse.

Her gaze swept over the remaining group, assessing for any signs of shock or distress. "Everyone else all right?"

One man stood apart, trembling visibly, even through his thick winter coat. "We're okay, I guess." He shoved his hands into his pockets, his attention drawn to the glittering shards of ice in the snow. "But this...I don't know how we'll come back from it. There's only two of us now."

Katherine pulled a peppermint out of her pocket and handed it to him to ease his shakes.

John stepped closer. "What do you mean? Where's Roger?"

"The Ice King?" Leia whispered to Katherine, who nodded, equally intrigued.

The man made a helpless gesture. "He's been MIA since Tuesday night. No plans, no ideas, not so much as a message." He jerked his thumb at his companion. "Larry here had to improvise. Everything's a mess. We've had to scrounge for equipment from other teams, and none of us knows what we're supposed to be doing."

Larry shifted his weight, looking lost among the icy debris.

Leia's gaze traced the jagged edges of broken ice. "Did you miscalculate while attaching a piece?"

Larry nudged a shard with his boot. "Looks like it," he mumbled, his voice barely audible over the wind. "This is all my fault."

"It'll be okay," Leia said, her tone gentle but firm. "Paul's in good hands. He'll be back before you know it. You've still got time."

"Time for what?" Larry gestured at the wreckage. "It's ruined. Shattered. We can't win now." His eyes darted to the crowd of onlookers surrounding their devastated camp.

His teammate's gloved hand landed on his back with a muffled thump. "Maybe not. But we'll face them in battle all the same."

Katherine wished there was something she could say to make it better.

Then Leia perked up. "What if you use the pieces? It's a bit like a shattered mirror." Her hands moved animatedly as she spoke. "Think *Alice Through the Looking Glass*. A giant Cheshire Cat on one side, Alice on the other. Nothing needs to be very tall. You wouldn't have to use the scaffolding if it's damaged."

Larry's jaw unclenched. He inhaled slowly, a spark kindling in his eyes. "That's...not half bad." He planted his hands on his hips, directing his attention to Leia. "How good are you with a chainsaw?"

"She's incredible, actually," Katherine answered for her. "But maybe we save the ice version for when I'm not already in medical-alert mode."

"Fair enough." Leia laughed. "This is what I get for telling Kat too many stories." She shifted. "Seriously, though, you guys have got this. I can't wait to see what you create."

Larry squared his shoulders. "We'll give it our all."

Back at the cabin, Katherine leaned against the closed door. "Well," she said, her lips quirking, "this vacation's off to an interesting start."

Leia sprawled on the couch, looking as wrung out as Katherine felt. Her boots had left twin puddles on the floor, but neither of them had the energy to care. "You were incredible out there. I mean, you've always been the one to take charge when things go sideways, but that..." She shook her head, searching for words. "That was something else. Zero to trauma nurse in two seconds flat."

Katherine shrugged, tugging off her hat and gloves. "I'm good in floods. Excellent in mudslides. Blizzards are my personal best." They landed with a wet thump on a nearby chair. "But a fall and probable broken arm is hardly extraordinary."

Leia shed her coat without budging from the couch, letting herself melt into the cushions. "Still, that was intense. He could've broken his neck, his back. Anything. Who knew watching ice sculpting could be so nerve-racking? One minute, it's all graceful art, and the next it's an extreme sport gone wrong."

Katherine perched on the arm of the sofa. "Imagine actually doing it."

"You won't let me," Leia said with a grin.

"Ha. True. But seriously, I guess for these sculptors, the passion outweighs the risk." Katherine went to investigate the welcome basket on the kitchen counter.

"Show me someone who doesn't love a chainsaw, and I'll show you someone who's never used one," Leia called after her.

"I'll take your word for it." Katherine rummaged through the basket, finding locally made chocolate-covered almonds, artisanal cheese, and what looked like homemade cookies. She grabbed the almonds—sugar and protein, perfect for post-adrenaline crashes. "Want some?"

CHAPTER FIVE 43

"Maybe later." Leia stared at the ceiling. "I just keep thinking how amazing it must be to have a passion like that. Even better, to have a job like yours that truly matters. You're there when people need you most."

Katherine's expression softened. "Your work is important, too." Leia had bounced through a few jobs over the years, but she'd put her heart and soul into every one of them. She'd started as a data analyst for the police department. She'd consulted for nonprofits on their impact metrics, and she'd even done a stint analyzing baseball statistics for the local minor league team, completely revamping their training program. And now, the newspaper. Leia was always looking for ways to make people's lives better, and Katherine admired her for it.

Leia's gaze remained fixed on the ceiling, her voice flattening. "I'm a fact-checker for a dying newspaper."

"Then you should check *your* facts." Katherine's nurse voice slipped out. But darn it, she couldn't help it. "You're a mathematical genius, a statistician, and an excellent analyst. You're a specialist in crime statistics. And what about last week? You worked with the Seattle city council and got the gun crime referendum through. How brilliant was that?"

Leia pushed herself up, tucking a wayward strand of hair behind her ear. "That was a good one, right?" A small smile played at the corners of her mouth. "I suppose you have a point. It's just..." She hesitated, her eyes meeting Katherine's. "Sometimes I wonder if I'm making a difference, you know? I spend so much time making sure every detail is lined up so that people know the truth, but I'm not sure all of them care."

"Enough do." She gave Leia's shoulder a squeeze. "The

truth is more important than ever these days. And trust me, everything we do adds up. Every fact you verify, every patient I bandage...it all contributes to the bigger picture. We're both making a difference."

Leia smiled. "What would I do without you?"

"Probably get into twice as much trouble with power tools." Katherine popped an almond into her mouth. "But good for you, you'll never have to find out."

Leia swiped an almond. "Mind if I grab a shower before dinner?"

Katherine waved her off. "Go ahead. I've got a date with Hercule Poirot." She patted the e-reader on the coffee table.

Leia scooped up her leopard-print satchel of lotions and potions and headed for the bathroom.

"Hey, Leia," Katherine called, wedging a pillow behind her back.

Leia paused at the threshold, looking back.

"What you did for Larry out there?" Katherine's fingers hovered over her e-reader. "Encouraging him to keep going. That was really something. Whatever they create now, it'll be because of you."

Leia stood a little straighter. "Thanks, Kat," she murmured before the bathroom door clicked shut.

❄

AN HOUR AND A HALF LATER, Katherine and Leia pushed through the heavy door of The Lumberjack's Lodge. The bustling steakhouse engulfed them in a warm gust of air and the rich aroma of grilled meat. The place was a living, breathing homage to Northern Minnesota's rugged charm. Rustic beams stretched overhead, adorned with vintage snowshoes and colorful fishing lures. Sepia-toned photographs on the walls chronicled the area's logging history, while antler chandeliers cast a golden glow over the bustling tables.

As they wove through the crowd, a familiar voice cut through the din. John's enthusiastic wave guided them to a cozy corner booth. Trishelle was already nursing a glass of iced tea, while John had a beer. In true Midwest fashion, the couple stood to greet them.

"Well, if it isn't our local hero," John said.

Heat crept up Katherine's neck. Before she could deflect, Trishelle enveloped them both in warm hugs that smelled like fresh snow and cedar.

"You really were something out there," John insisted.

Katherine slid into the booth beside Leia. "I just go where I'm needed."

"Maybe," he countered, settling in beside Trishelle, "but you won't say no to a free steak dinner. We insist."

Trishelle's eyes twinkled. "And you'll soon learn I always get my way."

Katherine tried—and failed—to hide her amusement. "Noted and logged for future reference."

"Kat's always been good at reading the room," Leia chimed in.

Trishelle leaned forward, elbows on the table. "So, you mentioned you and Katherine go way back. There must be stories."

Leia shot Katherine a playful look. "Oh, I've got plenty, but I'm not sure Kat's ready for me to spill all her secrets just yet."

Katherine rolled her eyes, fighting back a smile. "Let's just say Leia and I have weathered our fair share of storms together. But enough about us. How did you two lovebirds meet?"

John draped an arm around Trishelle. "Howard University. I was knee-deep in med school, while Trishelle was juggling psychology—"

"With music," Trishelle finished, eyes dancing.

"Right. I can't forget the music," John said, giving her a fond squeeze.

"Psychology and music?" Leia jumped in. "I fact-checked a story on that. Studies show music therapy can reduce anxiety in long-term medical patients."

Trishelle pointed at Leia with delight. "Exactly! At St. Paul's Children's Hospital, we've integrated music into our treatment programs. It's incredible how it helps the kids heal. You should see their faces—it gets me every time."

"At least twice a week," John said fondly.

*How sweet.* "Wow, Trishelle." She was just a ray of sunshine.

"It's beyond rewarding," she said. "Watching a child lose themselves in a song they've just learned or seeing them transported by a live performance—" She paused, glancing at John. "It's going to be lonely, though, with Rita retiring next year."

"Rita's your colleague who used to join you here," Katherine recalled from their first meeting.

"Yes, but she's not just a colleague," Trishelle said. "More like a partner in crime. Rita runs Family Support Services at the hospital, but we go way back. Like fifty years back. We met at a music camp as kids, if you can believe it."

"We can," Leia piped in.

"She was my maid of honor," Trishelle added. "And I was hers—the whole thing. When the job at Children's opened up, she all but strongarmed me into applying."

"Strongarmed?" John scoffed. "More like issued a royal decree."

Trishelle swatted his arm. "Oh, hush. Are you really complaining?"

"Only about the arctic expedition to shovel our driveway in winter." He caught her hand mid-swat, pressing it to his lips for a tender kiss. "But Minnesota's been good to us, snow and all."

A server approached, decked out in a red flannel shirt and a black toque. "Evening, folks. Drinks to start? Our local brews are legendary, and our cocktail menu will warm you right up."

Katherine scanned the drink menu while Leia read aloud with growing delight. "The Frostbite Martini. A wintery mix of vodka, white chocolate liqueur, peppermint schnapps, and half-and-half, served in a glass rimmed with crushed candy canes. It's like a Peppermint Patty grew up and got sassy."

"That's the kind of trouble I need in my life," Trishelle said. "I'll take one."

"Me too," Leia announced.

John shook his head. "I'll stick to my trusty IPA, but you ladies enjoy your liquid desserts."

"He says it like it's a bad thing," Trishelle mused.

"What pairs well with the special?" Katherine asked. The waiter almost dropped his pen.

"The...special?" he stammered. "The head cheese with lutefisk sauerkraut?"

"That's the one." Katherine hadn't had lutefisk since the International Trauma Nurses' conference in Oslo in '03. She hoped they made it just as good here. "It says it comes on a bed of polenta with grilled vegetables. Which vegetables are those?"

"I believe it's a mix of grilled bell peppers and tomatoes." He seemed to pull himself together, barely. "I'd suggest a strong bourbon to pair with it. The strongest we've got."

"Sounds good." She handed him the menu. "I'll take my bourbon straight."

"Of course you will," the waiter said before fleeing.

Meanwhile John and Trishelle gaped at her. "You know what head cheese is, right?" John asked.

Leia waved him off. "Oh, she knows. Never split a pizza with this one. Even going half-and-half is dangerous—the toppings migrate."

Katherine planted her elbows on the table. "Hey, this recipe has survived centuries. Why would you think it's bad?"

"Your faith in historical cuisine is both admirable and terrifying," John said, raising is glass.

She'd take it as a compliment.

After the rest of their drinks arrived, Trishelle leaned in. "So what lured you to the land of ice and snow?"

Katherine and Leia shared a look.

"Well, go back to kindergarten," Leia began. "There used to be three of us—Kat, me, and Jen. We were inseparable."

Katherine shared their story of friendship, loss, and the My Little Pony lunchbox that had led them to the ice hotel. Then it hit her. "You know, Leia, maybe this wasn't our idea at all. Digging into the wish box. Taking off for the ice hotel. Maybe Jen's up there right now, grinning like a fool, toasting the angels that we finally got around to it."

"That's exactly what she'd do," Leia said softly.

Trishelle pressed a hand to her heart. "She's definitely doing victory laps."

John raised his glass. "To friendships that stand the test of time."

Trishelle followed suit. "To Katherine and Leia and their box of adventures."

"And to new friends," Katherine added as the group clinked glasses.

The waiter set down their plates—placing Katherine's dish with visible trepidation. "Does everything look right?" he asked as if it were a loaded question.

She took a hearty sniff. Sure, head cheese looked like gelatinous slices of patchwork meat pulled from the head of a cow, but with the lutefisk sauerkraut, it tasted like succulent sweetbread, briny salt, and heaven.

"Any word on Paul?" Leia asked, digging into her steak. "That accident today was terrifying."

John sliced into his steak with surgical precision. "We ran into Ian earlier. Paul's got a cast, but he's okay. Eager to get back to work, though sculpting with one hand won't be easy."

Katherine sampled the head cheese, appreciating the bold, old-world flavors while ignoring John's horrified expression. It was just food. "That team can't catch a break." She kept Paul's equipment concerns to herself, not wanting to stir up trouble.

"Roger's going to blow a gasket when he finally shows," John said between bites.

"How common are accidents here?" Leia's fork paused in midair. "Is this the worst you've seen?"

A shadow crossed Trishelle's face. "We were there when Rebecca..."

"Rebecca Hardney?" Leia recalled the vibrant young woman from the book.

John set down his fork with a quiet clink. "Five years ago, a sculpture collapsed on her. It was catastrophic." His gaze grew distant. "Eric was giving a TV interview. Rebecca and Craig were working on the piece behind him. Everything seemed fine, and then it all came crashing down. Right there, live on air."

"That sound." Trishelle shivered. "Today brought it all back. Eric's pretty shaken."

"I can't even fathom," Leia said.

"How did he keep competing after what happened?" Katherine wondered. She'd seen plenty of people fall apart after accidents like that.

John took a long pull from his beer. "Rebecca's parents got him through it. The accident happened right as Eric was opening his restaurant in Dallas. The family rallied around him." He paused. "Talent-wise, he's right up there with the Ice King, but he hasn't won a competition since Rebecca's accident."

"Rebecca was Rita's only child," Trishelle whispered as John's hand found her back. "I was her godmother. We still come because this was her world."

"It's how we remember her," John added.

"That's beautiful," Leia said.

"So was she." Trishelle steadied herself. "Being here... sometimes I swear I can hear her laugh echoing off the ice."

"She is here," John said, his eyes filled with quiet certainty.

Trishelle squeezed his hand. "She'd be rolling her eyes and telling us to lighten up." A short laugh escaped her lips. "Heavens, she loved this place."

John turned to Katherine and Leia. "Her fellow ice artists never fail to amaze. The sculptures they create—it's like watching dreams take shape."

"I almost envy you seeing it fresh," Trishelle said, raising her glass. "To new adventures tonight."

"To Rebecca," Leia said, joining her in the toast.

"To her legacy," John said. "And your wish box."

Katherine clinked glasses with theirs. "In this magical realm Rebecca helped create and the wish box helped us find."

"To friends," Leia finished, summing it up perfectly.

# CHAPTER SIX

Leia stood in front of the mirror, assessing her reflection with a critical eye. She'd layered on her after-dinner going-out ensemble. A thermal base layer, *check*. A cozy sweater, puffy down vest, and a subzero parka, *check, check, and check*. The cold didn't stand a chance against her fleece-lined leggings topped with suddenly very tight jeans. She'd pulled on not one, but two pairs of wool socks before stuffing her feet into her heaviest boots.

"Do you think this is enough?" she asked, turning to face Kat, who leaned against the edge of the dresser, already geared up in her streamlined winter kit.

Kat's lips twitched. "I think you'll be plenty warm, but I'm worried you might tip over."

"Ha, ha." Well, she didn't have a compact arctic ensemble fit for a Himalayan medical camp.

Leia took an experimental step, feeling like a human marshmallow. "I'd rather not catch my death out there. The ice bar is kept at twenty-two degrees Fahrenheit."

"Trust me, you'll be fine," Kat said, standing. "Just

remember, if you start to feel dizzy, confused, or like your heart is racing, those could be signs of heat stroke."

Leia rolled her eyes but laughed. "Thanks, Dr. Kat."

They stepped out into the night and headed out toward the ice hotel, marveling at the way its walls glowed from within. True to form, they arrived a full half hour before the VIP party was set to start.

Arched wooden doors stood open in a thick wall of snow. As they pushed through the stiff, insulating plastic strips that shielded the entrance, Leia's breath caught in her throat. Even the normally unflappable Kat let out a soft gasp.

The lobby stretched before them, an enchanted forest of ice and snow. Delicate ice trees reached toward the high ceiling. Glittering frozen flowers bloomed on the walls, with playful fairies dancing among them. Lights embedded in the sculptures shifted from blue to pink to soft green, bringing the frozen wonderland to life.

A tinkling sound, like fairy music, filled the air as ice crystals brushed against each other. Above, a dazzling ice chandelier sparkled, each droplet a miniature work of art.

At the far end, a fairy ice queen sat regally on her throne, scepter held high, while an arch of snowflakes the size of dinner plates swirled toward the ceiling.

"It's a sign," Leia murmured.

"We're in the right place," Kat said.

They ventured deeper into the hotel, passing a few staff members making final adjustments to lighting and sound systems. The grand hall that opened before them could have been plucked from Mount Olympus itself. Towering ice columns, carved with scenes of gods and heroes, supported a vaulted ceiling that glittered like the night sky.

## CHAPTER SIX

If Zeus himself walked in, Leia wouldn't even have been surprised.

At the center, a massive ice bar rose from the snowy floor, shaped like a mountain and etched with lightning bolts. Zeus's throne, rendered in gleaming ice, crowned the peak. Upbeat music pulsed through the space, synchronized with dancing lights.

"I'm so glad we got here early." Kat rubbed her gloved hands together, then gasped. "Oh, my gosh. Take a right."

They zigzagged past an ice sculpture of Perseus battling Medusa, her snaky locks coiling above. Through an arched doorway, they entered a rectangular hall dominated by a colossal dragon sculpture.

The beast's scales shimmered in shades of blue and green, lit from within. Its glowing red eyes seemed to follow them as they explored.

Leia spotted an ice slide built into the dragon's back, complete with snow-sculpted stairs resembling piles of treasure. A teenage girl shrieked with delight as she zipped down, the walls swallowing her. Only her raised arms betrayed her glide down the ice.

Two more cheered for her at the bottom.

"Too bad we're too old for slides." Leia sighed.

"Are we?" Kat challenged.

"Race you to the top!" she said to a startled Kat before making a mad dash to the slide.

Well, more like a healthy jog.

"You're on." Kat tagged her on the arm as she whizzed past.

They clambered up the snowy stairs, giggling like schoolkids, out of breath and loving it. Leia pushed hard, the cold air burning her lungs, but Kat reached the summit first, plopping down onto the slide.

"You're a natural," Leia puffed, making it up the last few stairs.

"I think I broke my butt," Kat said before tipping off the edge, her laughter echoing as she zoomed down.

Leia caught her breath, eyeing the steep chute. She wasn't a teenager anymore, but...

Forget it.

She was doing it.

Leia sat a little—okay, a lot—more gingerly than Kat had. "Look out below!" she said, ready to thunder down the ice.

Instead, she inched along like a bead of water on a glass. Leia wiggled, trying to gain momentum. This was a mathematical problem, after all. Mass times acceleration equals force, and right now, despite her layers adding plenty of mass, her acceleration was practically zero. Her jeans created too much friction against the smooth ice.

"Come on, Leia! You can do it!" Kat called from the bottom.

"I am doing it!" Leia protested, scooting faster.

She bumped over a slight rise, seeing Kat's grin at the bottom. "There you are!"

"I think I'm going to need a spatula to get down this thing," Leia called, sweat trickling down her spine. Her layers had become a personal sauna.

"It'll pick up," Kat promised.

It didn't. Leia trickled all the way down, taking advantage of the situation by making it look like a daring, amazing, slow-motion shot as she sputtered to the bottom. "Ta-da," she announced, arms spread wide.

Kat pulled Leia to her feet as they both dissolved into giggles. "Who needs speed when you have style?" She brushed stray ice crystals from Leia's parka.

## CHAPTER SIX

"I'm just earning my drink at the bar," Leia shot back, checking her watch. They were still early. "Next time, I'm wearing a garbage bag and snow pants instead of jeans."

Kat laughed. Leia hadn't realized how much she'd missed goofing off. Then Kat's expression shifted, and she followed her friend's gaze to a lanky man hunched over the tail of the dragon slide.

His hands worked deftly, repairing a chipped section. A spiderweb tattoo peeked from the collar of his heavy work jacket.

"Yikes." Kat tensed, watching his hands.

"What?" He had a second tattoo on his left wrist, five dots arranged like pips on a die.

Kat's forehead creased as she took Leia's hand and tugged her toward the exit.

"Wait. Hold up." When did Kat get so judgy about a little ink? She used to worship Guns N' Roses when she and Kat were in middle school. Kat had even wanted to marry Axl Rose.

Besides—she freed herself from her friend's grip—it wasn't as if Kat even knew him. They were here for an adventure, and she wanted to meet this mysterious sculptor.

"Excuse me," Leia called, crunching over the snow. "Everything okay with our dragon friend?"

The man's dark eyes met Leia's, cold and assessing before warming with a practiced smile. "Just a run-in with one of the bartenders," he said, his voice deep and gravelly. "A few of them got a little too excited about the slide before we opened." He rubbed his hands together before pulling his gloves back on.

"Leia, let's head into the bar," Kat coaxed as if Leia had missed the first hint.

Leia stepped closer to admire his work. "I'm Leia, by the way. And this is my friend Katherine."

"Carlos," the man replied, shaking Leia's hand. His grip was firm, his voice controlled.

"You from around here, Carlos?" Kat asked, her tone clipped.

Carlos turned a cool gaze on her. "Nah, I'm from Boston."

Kat nodded stiffly. Leia shot her a questioning look, which Kat ignored.

*What is up with her?*

A petite woman with short, spiky hair under a slouched crochet beanie bounded up, her bangs artistically slicked to one side. She threw her arms around Carlos's neck. "There you are," she exclaimed, kissing his cheek. "I've been looking all over for you."

Carlos softened, pulling her close. "Just fixing up the dragon," he explained. "Leia, Katherine, this is Amy. She's the mastermind behind this whole thing."

Amy beamed at the compliment, her cheeks already pink from the cold. "Pleasure to meet you both. The dragon here, heck, this whole room, was practice for the sea serpent we're working on for the competition."

"I saw that today," Leia said, remembering. "The scales were beautiful."

Amy ducked her head. "We think we have the dragon nailed, but the mermaids...they're tricky. I've spent six months on the design, and the balance is still off."

"If you can make that dragon slide, you can do anything," Leia insisted.

"So you liked the slide?" Amy grinned.

"It was an experience like no other," Leia said. "I can't imagine the skill it takes to create something like this."

Amy shrugged, pleased. "It's a team effort. And I'm lucky to have Carlos. He's a brilliant artist himself."

Carlos ducked his head. "Amy's the real talent. She gave me a chance when no one else would," he added, eyeing Kat.

Kat cleared her throat. Leia didn't know what was going on, but she was determined to smooth things over.

"Did you see the accident today?" she blurted. Maybe not the best icebreaker, but she was winging it. "I hope there's a way for the team to recover."

"Not with Roger MIA," Carlos snipped.

Amy's face fell, worry flickering in her eyes. "This is so unlike Roger. He's always been competitive, but this event? It's everything to him."

"To a fault," Carlos growled.

Amy winced. "To be honest, Roger can be a jerk about it sometimes. But he's harmless."

"Unless he feels like he's not going to win." Carlos's jaw tightened as he busied himself replacing the barrier ropes around the dragon's tail. "I should get back to the competition site," he muttered, slamming one of the clips into a latch with barely contained fury. "Make sure everything's on track."

Amy nodded, watching as he stalked away.

"He's not usually this angry." She forced a smile. "It's not Carlos's fault." She crossed her arms, almost hugging herself. "After the accident in Roger's camp, we did a safety check. It wasn't good. We found problems with our rigging and had to take everything down. I've never seen anything like it."

"Rigging—like for lifting the ice?" Leia asked. This was all so new to her.

"Exactly." Amy squared her shoulders but couldn't

hide her trembling hands. "If we'd tried using those rigs —" She shook her head. "I could have ended up like Rebecca. Now we're behind, and I don't know how we'll catch up."

"That's awful." No wonder Carlos was edgy. "Was it the straps?"

Amy stared at her, the color draining from her face. "How did you know?"

"Just guessing," Leia said quickly, not wanting to upset her further.

"I bought all new straps for this competition." Amy jammed her hands in her pockets. "When we inspected them today, four of them were frayed inside the buckle casing. They could have snapped at any moment." She shuddered. "Sorry. It's just..."

"Scary," Leia finished. "Has this happened before?"

"Not to us. We all guard our equipment pretty carefully. Roger's paranoid about it." She gave a humorless laugh. "This is the first time I've had issues. Maybe I've never been this close to winning before."

Wait. If someone was targeting champions like that... "Rebecca's accident was an accident, right? Did anyone check the straps holding the ice block that killed her?"

Amy's face fell. "We shouldn't talk about that."

"I'm sorry," Leia immediately offered. "I didn't mean to upset you. I just think someone could have—"

"Rebecca's accident was different," Amy cut in. "The blocks were already stacked and stable. There was no rigging involved. Just saws and chisels at that point." Her mouth tightened. "Equipment didn't cause that collapse. It's easy to make a mistake if your head's not in the right place. It wasn't anyone's fault."

"Not everything's a conspiracy," Leia agreed. "But

seeing all this passion and artistry, it's hard to understand why anyone would want to ruin it."

Amy's gaze went distant, frost glinting in her spiky hair. "Some people would do anything to win."

Just then, John and Trishelle burst in, cheeks flushed and eyes sparkling. "Leia!" They were with a couple Leia didn't recognize, but John's backslapping and Trishelle's arm-linking showed they were old friends.

She watched Amy slip away. Maybe they could talk more later.

"Katherine, where's Katherine?" John called, waving her over. "Allow me to introduce Mark and Lisa. They're in cabin one, celebrating this guy's big 5-0."

Mark gave a mock bow, his silver-streaked hair and the laugh lines around his eyes lending him a distinguished air. "With age comes wisdom."

"And chocolate," Lisa, a petite blonde woman, added. "Our friends from Kanabec keep sending gift baskets to our room. They'll bury us in truffles."

"My favorite," Mark said. "Along with hazelnut pralines, salted caramel dark chocolate bark, peanut butter cups, chocolate-dipped strawberries..."

"In short, the party's in our cabin," Lisa said.

"Well, happy birthday, Mark," Kat said, her usual warmth returning. "How about we all grab a drink to celebrate? My treat."

Leia trailed behind the others, keeping an eye out for either Amy or Carlos. Although she had a feeling they were long gone.

She still didn't understand why Kat had been so standoffish with Carlos. Kat could be brusque, but she'd been edging on rude for no apparent reason. Then Carlos had left abruptly at the mention of the Ice King. And poor Amy had been the victim of sabotage. Her words about being pitted against the other competitors felt ominous.

A glittering ice lake relief adorned the wall to the right of the Medusa and Perseus archway. Fantastical fish poked their heads from the rippling surface, leading the way to the man behind the bar.

He was younger, with a shock of vivid blue hair and a jacket to match. "Welcome to the ice bar," he said, resting his gloved hands on the frozen surface. "What can I get you fine folks tonight?"

They placed their orders and soon held cups made of ice, filled with brightly colored drinks that glowed like the walls around them.

"This way." Trishelle led them to a cozy nook. Ice benches topped with fur surrounded a gas fire. The flickering flames cast a warm shimmer over their faces but gave off no actual heat.

"To the big 5-0," Kat said, lifting her glass.

Lisa joined her. "We picked a great way to celebrate. We've come up for the day to see the competition before, but this is our first time staying in the hotel. We're so excited," she said, clinking ice cups with everyone before settling back down. "We should have gotten here earlier. Looks like there's a lot of drama this year."

"Roger usually saves his drama for the competition," Mark said. "He lives and breathes for this stuff. I can't fathom what he's gaining from his disappearing act."

"Maybe he is having trouble coming up with a design," Leia suggested. "They seem complicated." Amy had clearly put months of thought into hers, while Roger's team appeared rudderless.

John shook his head. "Roger always has a plan. He was all fired up about the theme for this year's competition when they announced it last year. Tales of Gods and Heroes. It was right up his alley." He leaned forward. "Roger usually haunts this place. Especially on opening night. He likes to see people admiring his work. The only time he's missed a second of the competition was two years ago, but he was only out for the first day."

"Where did he go?" Leia asked. If she were a competitor on a timeline, it would take something catastrophic to drag her away. Especially with a prize on the line.

Trishelle made a noise like someone was about to spill some tea.

John leaned in. "I don't know where he went or who he went with, but when he came back, he looked like someone had put his face through a meat grinder."

Lisa winced. "He still looked horrible at the awards ceremony four days later. Black eye, split lip, the works. Everyone assumed he took a chunk of ice to the face."

"More like a few fists," John mumbled on the edge of his ice cup.

Kat lowered her drink. "Someone beat him up?"

"Sure looked that way." Mark swirled the dregs in his drink cup before finishing it off. "Kind of difficult to punch yourself in the face that hard. But he wouldn't admit to who did it, even though whoever it was probably would have gone to jail for felony assault."

Trishelle shuddered, pressing closer to John's side. "I can't imagine who would do something like that. I mean, I know it gets intense around here, but it never goes that far."

"Until it does," John said solemnly.

"No one around here would be capable of that kind of brutality," Lisa concluded with a nervous laugh. "This is Minnesota."

"Does anyone know what Carlos went to prison for?" Kat asked, her voice cutting through the air like a blade.

Leia nearly dropped her ice cup. By the looks of the faces around the fire, she wasn't the only one shocked.

"I've seen tattoos like his before," Kat told them. "He's done hard time."

Before anyone could speculate further, Ian approached with an infectious energy, his voice taking on the enthusiasm of a circus ringmaster. "Evening, folks! Just wanted to let you know the rest of the hotel is now open for you to explore."

Trishelle sprang from her seat. "Let's go."

"Great idea," John said, joining her.

Lisa popped up awkwardly. "Mark and I have a deluxe suite with a private hot tub. I can't wait to find out who carved the room. We told them we wanted the theme to be a surprise."

"Us too," John said. "We love surprises, and hot tubs."

"I didn't even realize we could learn our room theme," Leia said. Everything had been so last minute.

"We might not have had a choice," Kat said. "In any case, I like surprises."

Trishelle beckoned to Leia. "Are you coming?"

"Yes, of course." She'd been looking forward to this. Yet she couldn't shake the feeling that beneath the beauty and wonder of the ice hotel, there was a crack in the foundation.

Roger getting beat up during a competition. Amy's admission that someone was tampering with straps. Add in the accident that had claimed Rebecca, and the one she'd seen today. Leia's job was to look at facts and numbers, to find patterns. She prided herself on digging until she knew the truth.

Now her trusty BS radar was screaming.

## CHAPTER SIX

Kat rubbed her neck thoughtfully, where her long, ridiculous earrings touched the skin below her jaw. Leia knew that look. Kat was probably on the same track.

Kat might not spend her days like Leia did—looking for missteps, chasing down lies and correcting them, but Kat could read a room better than anyone.

Ian pulled open the wooden entry doors. The insulating plastic flaps swung from the ceiling, inviting them inside. "Ready for this?" he teased.

Leia took a deep breath, the icy air sharp in her lungs. For the first time in a long time, she didn't know what she was stepping into, but she wasn't going to let a single detail slip past her. "I'm ready."

## CHAPTER SEVEN

Katherine ventured into the newly unveiled section of the ice hotel, curiosity piqued. The snowy hallway stretched before her, lined with curtained rooms that beckoned to be explored.

But her mind buzzed with more than the allure of snow art. More than the colorful drinks and the fine company. She was still stuck on Carlos's prison tattoos, Roger's mysterious disappearance, and the hushed conversations about his brutal beating two years earlier. Not to mention the way Amy had cornered Leia.

She buried her hands in her pockets, her long earrings swaying as she shook her head. None of it sat right. None of it had been explained to her satisfaction.

And then there was Trishelle's recent offhand comment: *Rebecca put her heart and soul into everything she designed*.

No doubt the other artists were the same. For them, sculpting was a calling—just like medicine was for her. She couldn't imagine doing anything else. The only difference was her heart and soul weren't etched on the walls for everyone to see. And in that moment, she knew what she had to do—she'd try to understand the artists through their art.

The others might overlook the details, but Katherine wouldn't.

She couldn't.

The crisp, cold air nipped at her skin, but determination kept her warm as the group trailed Ian, their footsteps crunching on the snowy floor.

"Wander and explore." Ian's voice echoed slightly before the snow absorbed it. "Everything's open tonight, but tomorrow, only those with room reservations can stay past nine."

"Sounds good," Katherine said to herself.

One night was all she'd need.

"I'm impressed enough with the hallway." Leia halted at a mural of a whimsical underwater scene. A striped beachball sailed over the ocean waves, kicked by a majestic whale's gracefully arching tail.

"Larry's creation." Ian lifted the curtain on the doorway beyond. "As is this room."

Katherine spotted a placard next to the velvet curtain, covered in a sheet of clear ice.

*Room 1*

*Wanderlust by Larry Danvers*

An ice bench stood just inside the door, masterfully crafted to resemble vintage suitcases complete with travel tags and clasps. Stacked ice suitcases formed a charming table.

She moved deeper into the room, her gaze drawn to the walls, where a magnificent pirate treasure map had been carved into the tall, arched surface. It showcased a remote island surrounded by sea creatures. Illuminated from behind, it cast an easy glow, highlighting the skull and crossbones above and the bright red X marking the spot.

Leia ran her hand along the icy blocks surrounding a wooden platform that supported the mattress. "When we signed up for this, I thought we'd be sleeping in a snowy cave, not something like this." The headboard had been carved like a compass. Behind it, cut into the snowy wall, was a stunning representation of a sextant surrounded by a rainbow of glittering stars.

Trishelle beamed from the doorway. "I like Larry's style."

"Quirky and talented." John squeezed past her.

Katherine spotted a cackling monkey in the corner, hiding a stolen gold doubloon. "It's like stepping into an adventure novel."

Leia eyed the plain foam mattress on the plywood platform, surrounded by carved ice. "How are we going to stay warm when we sleep?"

"Subzero sleeping bags," Ian said. "Pillow included. Just snuggle in, zip up, and you're good until morning."

"I like it," Katherine said. They should be nice and cozy.

Leia raised a hand. "Where are the bathrooms?"

That was a good question. This was one big room, and the only door led to the hall.

"Most people go before they leave the cabins or lodge," Ian explained, "but there are heated port-a-potties at the end of each hall near the exits."

Katherine would be sure to arrive empty.

Leia craned her head back to check out the fist-sized hole in the tall, arched snow ceiling. She was no construction expert, but she would have avoided a hole in the roof. "I hope we don't get snowed on."

Ian gestured upward. "That's for ventilation. To prevent your breath from icing the walls."

*Wouldn't want anything to get icy in an ice hotel.* Still, the fresh air would be nice. She was glad the rooms wouldn't get stuffy.

Leia bent to inspect the gas fireplace between the ice luggage and the bed. "If our room is half this fun, I'll be in heaven."

"Let's go now." Ian moved toward the door.

"In a second." Katherine wasn't quite ready to leave treasure island. She wanted to know who Larry was. What did this room say about him? Her fingers hovered above the carvings along the wall bases—sea creatures and buried treasure with details as precise as anatomical drawings, from the scientifically accurate scales on a mermaid's tail to the perfectly proportioned coins spilling from a treasure chest.

Ian turned toward the rest of the group, who had migrated into the hall. "Call me if you need me. I think Mark has a question."

"John was right," Leia said, admiring a whimsical scene etched into the wall opposite the map. A hot-air balloon, seemingly crafted from a patchwork of quilts and textured fabrics, soared through a sky of smiling clouds. In the basket, hedgehogs wore tiny aviator goggles and scarves. They clinked miniature cups of hot cocoa, their spiky coats rendered with mathematical precision. "Larry's talent is unreal. I mean, hedgehogs in goggles. Who would have thought?"

Katherine joined her. "He was worried about competing without Roger, but it seems he's more than capable on his own." Larry clearly appreciated whimsy. The room struck her as innocently playful in a way that felt genuine. Yet every bit of it was practiced, exacting.

Interesting.

"Come on," Leia said. "Let's catch up with the group."

They exchanged knowing looks as they stepped back into the hallway. The group had ventured far ahead, their voices faint in the distance.

But then Leia's attention snagged on a carving in the hallway, just before another curtained door. "This is different."

It featured sharp, precise interlocking triangles. "This has to be one of Roger's rooms."

"You got it." Leia pointed to the plaque near the curtain.

*Room 2*

*The Mousetrap by Roger Cullins*

Leia lifted the curtain. "Let's see what the Ice King has to show us."

They stepped into a cat-and-mouse-themed room. The ice sculpture bench and table were carved into simple wedges of cheese, lacking the complexity Katherine had expected from Roger's work.

"It's cute," Leia offered. But her heart wasn't in her words.

"I can see where he was going." Katherine noted the cheese-wedge headboard on the bed, the cheese plate on the tall arched wall, and the giant mousehole on the opposite wall.

"The theme is very consistent." Leia's words held the same flat tone she used when she'd picked the wrong wall color. "I could never make a cheese-shaped ice bed."

The technical execution was flawless, every cheese hole defined. But after Larry's room, it felt plain. Boring. It was... cheese. Nothing more.

Was Katherine spoiled already?

No, she didn't think so. The room just lacked Larry's whimsical touches.

"We can't expect everything Roger does to be as gravity-defying as his competition sculptures," she reasoned.

"Maybe he wanted to try something different," Leia suggested, already heading for the hall.

Katherine frowned at the obvious triangle formed by the cheese wedge behind the bed. "I was really looking forward to a puzzle." For someone known for complexity, Roger's hidden triangle was surprisingly unhidden.

In the hallway, Leia drew close, her voice dropping to a whisper. "Is it me, or was that kind of weird?"

Katherine nodded, an uneasy feeling settling in her gut. "It's art, but..." She paused, mentally cataloging the discrepancies like symptoms. "The lack of apparent effort, the simplistic design—it doesn't line up with the reality-warping skill John described. I mean, this guy is a four-time winner. He's known for his detail work and competitive drive."

"So what was he thinking back there?"

There was no telling. Granted, the rooms weren't part of the competition, but her experience with Leia's DIY passion projects alone taught her one consistent truth—genuine creativity wasn't something you could switch off. Even her simplest projects—from her built-in reading nook with twinkle lights to her vintage door headboard—carried her signature style.

Katherine planted her hands on her hips. The absence of Roger himself was another red flag. She'd started exploring these rooms hoping to understand each artist. Instead, Roger's room had only deepened the mystery.

"Oh, look. Here's a room by Alexi," Leia said, coaxing the curtain aside.

*Room 3*

*The Throne Room by Alexi Karpotov*

This one made Katherine stop cold. A magnificent ice sculpture bench and table stood along the back wall, carved to resemble a royal throne and a banquet table laden with frozen delicacies. The bench boasted diamond-patterned stitching and regal emblems, while the table featured a stunning ice swan centerpiece on a platter.

Snow carvings transformed the walls into royal gardens.

Leia circled the ice bed. "Oh my gosh, look at this." The headboard was carved like a towering castle wall, complete with battlements and turrets. A vast and sweeping landscape stretched out behind it, depicting snowcapped mountains, frozen lakes, and ancient forests.

"Alexi has outdone himself," Katherine said.

"I feel like I should bow," Leia joked as she gestured to the throne.

"Now I really don't get the cheese," Katherine mused as they headed back into the hall. "Larry's room shows his adventurous spirit and humor. Alexi's room screams grandiose ambition and mastery. But the four-time champion's design tells us nothing. Except that he might be craving cheddar."

Leia dropped her voice. "I keep thinking about Amy. She made it sound like each of them were out for blood to win the contest. She had no reason to lie. In fact, I think she said more than she'd planned after Carlos's temper rattled her."

Katherine's mouth formed a thin line. "I'm not surprised he has a temper." Poor Amy. "It'll be interesting to see her room."

"And Carlos's, if he did one." Leia halted mid-step. "Speak of the devil. Here's his room."

Katherine's shoulders tensed. "We have to go in, don't we?" She wasn't sure she was ready to see inside his mind.

"Come on." Leia dragged her inside.

*Room 4*

*Open Air by Carlos Flores*

The splendor of the outdoor theme caught Katherine by surprise. The ice sculpture bench and table, carved to resemble a fallen log and tree stump, had surfaces textured like rough bark. Life-size ice sculptures of a fox and a rabbit played tag next to the log bench.

Leia examined a wall depicting a lush forest scene, complete with towering evergreens and woodland creatures. "Amazing, isn't it?" Her finger traced the trajectory of a brook winding through the trees, its icy surface glinting in the soft light. "Carlos has a real talent for bringing the outdoors inside."

Katherine studied the opposite wall, where a stag commanded a clearing, its antlers stretching toward the snowy ceiling. The complete nature fantasy made her wonder. "Do you think his time in prison inspired him to see nature this way?"

Leia paused. "It's possible, but you know, we shouldn't get blinded by assumptions. People can surprise you."

"I'm only focusing on what might have been on his mind." Katherine's attention caught on a crushed flower sprouting new growth in the corner.

"He's hard to read," Leia said, looking closely at the flower. "I know Amy relies on him."

"True," Katherine conceded. They didn't know much about Carlos, Amy, or her taste in men. "It's just... You're going to call me crazy, but after today's accident, I can't help but wonder if somebody's trying to sabotage the competition."

"I was thinking the same thing." Leia's forehead creased as she examined the bed's headboard, carved to resemble a craggy cliff with a waterfall cascading down, frozen mid-flow. "The buckle break in Roger's camp today was no accident. Someone manipulated the spring. I saw it."

Katherine froze. "Are you sure?"

Leia nodded grimly. "They levered something into it. I saw the marks. Then they twisted the spring out."

"Unbelievable." Katherine rested her hands on her hips, trying to think.

"Then Amy told me that she and her team inspected their straps after what happened to Paul, and her straps were also frayed inside the buckle."

Katherine stared at her.

"I swear," Leia said. "And get this. Amy had just bought those straps brand new."

Wow. Katherine dropped her hands. "When were you going to tell me this?"

Leia's voice stayed low. "I needed privacy first."

Good point. Katherine's mind assembled the diagnostic timeline. "So first, ice falls on Eric's wife."

"Five years back," Leia noted.

Katherine ran a hand through her hair. "And Eric hasn't won since."

"I actually talked to Amy about that." Leia shoved her hands into her pockets. "According to her, Rebecca's accident was different. They were already in the carving stage. The ice was stacked and stable. There was no rigging involved, no straps. Just saws and chisels." She frowned. "We can't rule out sabotage, but it doesn't fit the pattern. Amy's convinced it was an accident."

"Then let's go back to Roger's team," Katherine said. Leia's revelation had her thinking about everything in a completely different light. "Paul told me someone had loosened their straps twice early this week. If Roger's the favorite to win..." She hesitated. "He might very well have a target on his back."

Leia fiddled with her earring. "Maybe he's dealing with an emergency or throwing a creative tantrum, but I agree. His absence feels strange."

"If someone was trying to undermine the competition, could they have figured out a way to keep Roger away?"

Katherine left the darker possibility unspoken.

"We'll keep our eyes open," Leia promised. "He has to turn up eventually."

True. "Maybe today's accident will bring him around."

"About that." Leia's voice dropped lower. "We know the collapse today wasn't an accident. Someone used something sharp to weaken the buckle on the straps in both Roger's and Amy's camps." She shook her head. "That's so risky. These people depend on their tools, and it's easy to damage them. My biggest project right now is a bird backsplash, and I'd still never let anyone mess with my sharps."

"Wait. Are you serious?"

"Dead serious. Have you ever known a crafter who lets anyone touch their scissors?"

"You're the only crazy crafter I know."

"Sharp edges are a pain in the rear if they go dull or break. It's the same for tools, only more expensive to fix. Let me put it this way. If I break a sharp, I'm out a lot of cash. If one of them does it here, they're out of the competition. Maybe out of the industry altogether. Everyone would know they were the one shoving their sharps into other people's buckles."

"Bent tools tell all the tales," Katherine said.

"You think you're being cute, but you're right. It's not like there's a hardware store anywhere around here, even if regular stores carried these kinds of tools. And forget about stealing one. Everyone guards their equipment like gold, and not only because they know someone is messing with their stuff. We're in the middle of nowhere, and if something goes missing, you're in trouble."

"I hadn't thought of that, but you're right." Katherine stole one last glance at Carlos's nature paradise before heading out into the hall. "I thought I was the one who grew up on Nancy Drew."

"I borrowed them," Leia said, fighting her way through the curtain to join her friend.

"There you are," Trishelle called down to them. She leaned out of a doorway at the far end of the hall, right before it broke off in two directions. "Come see the workshop. We're all in here."

Leia turned to Katherine. "Shoot," she whispered. "I wanted to find our room."

"Same. We'll make it quick."

Ian beckoned them inside the large workshop. Packed snow walls featured framed photographs of builders in bright coveralls constructing the hotel with powerful backhoes and snow-making machines.

"Join us." Trishelle motioned them toward John, Mark, and Lisa, who were clustered near a waist-high wall made of clear ice blocks that separated the front display area from the rest of the workshop. A flimsy yellow chain stretched across the gap.

"Just a sec," Leia said, sticking close to Katherine. She blinked at the long workshop tables littered with ice picks, axes, and dozens of tools. "Maybe it wouldn't be so hard to grab a spare after all."

Katherine's jaw nearly dropped as she surveyed the room. There wasn't just one loose tool—they were everywhere. Hanging from the walls, scattered across benches, propped up against ice blocks. Chisels, saws, hammers, and implements she couldn't begin to name.

Where there weren't tools, there were keys, a whole pegboard filled with tagged keys on upturned nails, labeled for bobcats and boom lifts. It was organized chaos.

Ian beamed at their interest. "Isn't it great? We have everything you'd need to break ice, stack ice, and carve it."

Or destroy it. And no one could ever pin it back on you.

Katherine braced a hip against the half-wall, studying a particularly wicked-looking ice saw. But it wasn't the saw that made her heart drop. On a nearby pegboard hung a chisel with a bent tip. Neon fibers clung to the frost on its edge.

She pointed it out to Leia and watched her friend's face fall.

There was a saboteur.

## CHAPTER
# EIGHT

Leia drummed her fingers against her leg as she stared at the chisel with the bent tip.

*Relax. Focus. Think.*

A lot of the tools in the workshop were banged up. Four of the teeth on the ice saw were bent. A rusty stain clung to a prong of one of the ice clamps. As far as the chisel? It was small, sharp, and the right width to lever into a buckle and do damage. And Leia knew for a fact using it that way could have bent the tip.

But...

Leia stared at the plethora of tools on the wall. The large flathead screwdriver, several of the drill bits, especially the ones designed to bore holes in the ice, or even the hanging pry bar could all easily bust the spring in a buckle and then fray a strap to ribbons.

"Don't get ahead of yourself," she murmured.

She was not a crime lab.

Kat turned. "Did you say something?"

"No." Leia waved a hand. Nothing she'd like to share.

Yet.

People saw her pink hair, her crazy parrot, and her affinity for wearing the gaudiest earrings money could buy, and assumed she was impulsive. Her friendly Midwest nature didn't help—talk first, think later was practically her motto. But when it came down to it, she'd always been both meticulous and careful. It was what drew her to her line of work.

Details mattered. Getting them right mattered. Presenting them correctly so people could discern reality mattered. That was why Leia would rather be certain before voicing her deepest thoughts. Still, the pieces were aligning, forming a pattern she couldn't ignore.

A deadly accident five years ago.

Multiple artists with damaged equipment.

Roger's assault two years ago.

Paul's accident today.

She chewed her lip. Someone could be threatening Roger again, forcing him to stay away from the competition.

"Slow down, Sherlock." It was pure speculation. Someone had sabotaged Roger's team after he left. Maybe they'd needed him gone first. But if that chisel had damaged Amy's equipment... Leia suppressed a shiver. The ice could have killed her.

She needed proof before anyone else got hurt. Her math geek friends always joked about false correlations—pool the wrong data sets and suddenly you could prove an international pirate shortage caused global warming. "Arrrgh."

"Okay, that one I definitely heard." Kat moved closer. "What's up?"

"I swear I wasn't being a pirate," Leia muttered.

"What?"

Leia flashed a rueful smile. "I need to know how unusual it would be for competitors to be in this area. Would someone grabbing a tool off the pegboard raise any red flags?"

She shifted her attention to Ian. "I can't get over your setup. The drill for the ice cups—it's all hand-cranked, right? Anything that uses battery packs would be too unreliable. The cold must do a number on the charge." She examined the drill closer. "And what about ice buildup? Does it cause binding? Do people come in for replacements when their tools act up?"

"The cups are hand-cranked every night, we use special lubricants, and people come in all the time," Ian said. "If your tools fail while working, someone could get hurt."

"We know all about that," Kat stated plainly, her voice grave.

Leia froze on the spot. *Careful, now*. No sense letting everyone know they were suspicious.

Kat had the subtlety of a sledgehammer.

Leia turned to the group, throwing a thumb over her shoulder at Kat. "I shoot a staple gun into my own hand *one time*, and she never lets me forget it."

Kat's eyes jumped. Good. She'd realized they needed to put on a show to cover her slip.

"Oh, please, the staple gun was just the beginning." She tossed her hands up. "Do I need to mention the debacle with the sander?"

Low blow. Leia bit back a laugh despite the tension. "I was eight! No one told me to check my shoelaces!"

Trishelle barked out a laugh. "Some things you don't forget."

"Like the time Kat glued her own butt to the homecoming float senior year," Leia added. Two could play at this game.

John doubled over laughing while Trishelle traded a grin with Kat. "Hand to heaven, that would be me, too."

"Don't be scared, folks. Come on in," Ian said, beckoning the guests at the door. "We're just talking about how we built this place."

While Ian launched into his spiel, Kat pulled Leia aside. "We need to talk."

"Later," Leia murmured, watching Ian direct the latest guests to the colorful construction photos. She needed to understand what could have happened before the competition even started. "Ian," she called out, "what's the trickiest part about building an ice hotel?"

"The weather's the killer." Ian peeled off his gloves. "And most unpredictable. It has to be cold enough for the snow machines to make snow, but warm enough so the snow's heavy. That makes it pack well on the frames we use for the rooms."

Leia studied the ceiling, mentally deconstructing it. "How many frames do you have?"

"Not many." Ian stuffed his gloves in his back pocket. "We keep scooting them down as we go, packing more snow on top to make long corridors. Then we use wood forms for the front and back walls, cutting each long tube into sections like a loaf of bread. Pack the snow in, take the form down, and there's your room."

Interesting. "The walls have different thicknesses?"

Ian nodded. "Artists use that in sculpting. Rooms between corridors can have deep relief because the walls are up to eight feet thick. We use chainsaws to cut the doors."

Practical and ingenious. Two of Leia's favorite things.

## CHAPTER EIGHT

"So all we needed for our snow fort was a frame to use as a mold," Kat said, giving Leia space to investigate. Kat always had her back like that.

"Then maybe we would have had a roof that didn't collapse," Leia added.

"On second thought, nah." Kat snorted. "It wouldn't have changed a thing."

True. If they'd managed to keep a roof up at all, their shenanigans would have brought it down eventually.

Lisa ran a finger over the ice-block divider. "What happens when spring comes? Do you just let it melt?"

"We knock it down with a bulldozer." Ian glanced ruefully at the perfectly pitched ceiling. "It takes months to create a masterpiece and only hours to smash it into oblivion."

Leia winced. Then again, she was the one who refused to take down her Lego buildings until she ran out of bricks to build new ones.

"Want to see more?" Kat asked. "Or do you have more questions?"

"I'm good. Let's explore." Leia turned to Ian with a grateful smile. "Thanks. This place is so much more than I imagined."

The corners of his eyes crinkled with pleasure. "Thanks for coming. I'm always around if you have questions."

As they turned to leave, Trishelle and John took their place with Ian. Lisa and Mark had other plans.

"Come see our room," Lisa urged. "They pulled out all the stops."

"It's ridiculous," Mark agreed.

"We would, but we're dying to see ours," Kat said.

"You haven't yet?" Lisa gushed. "We saw it on the way down. It's one of the Ice King's rooms, and it's amazing."

"Don't tell them the theme. It's too cool," Mark said, nudging her.

"Go the opposite way out of the workshop—halfway down that hall on the left." Lisa entwined her hand with her husband's.

"Thanks!" Leia said, already on her way.

The moment they were out of earshot, Kat turned to her. "Is the chisel proof of sabotage?"

"I don't know." Leia lowered her voice. "I'm afraid to read too much into it. Almost every tool in there was beat up, and more than one could have damaged those straps. It isn't necessarily proof." Though she noted it. And that fiber on the edge was suspicious. Chisels were for ice, not fibers.

"Who do you think is causing all this trouble?" Kat whispered. "Who wants to win that bad?"

A large man in a bright red parka pushed past them. "Excuse me, ladies," he mumbled through his scarf.

They shouldn't be talking in the open like this.

Amy was already so upset. Feeding into suspicion and paranoia would only make the competitors more edgy. And as Amy pointed out, when people's heads weren't right, bad things happened.

"We'll keep our eyes open. Hopefully nothing else goes wrong." Leia gestured down the hall. "For now, let's have some fun. I can't wait to see what the Ice King did with our room."

Kat shot her a conspiratorial grin. "What if it's entirely dedicated to sausages?"

Leia snorted. "That would be hysterical, actually. We'd certainly have something to tell Charley."

"She'd be disappointed she couldn't steal one.'"

"You know, the Ice King did more than one room. Maybe he saved the best for last. Our room could be a mind-blowing masterpiece." Leia shrugged a shoulder. "Mark and Lisa seemed impressed. Or it could be another giant wedge of cheese. Either way, it'll be memorable."

"There's only one way to find out." They set off down the snowy hallway, and in about two seconds, Leia found herself torn between examining the carved walls and the excitement of hurrying to where they wanted to go.

They passed a stunning *Mona Lisa*, then a geometric pattern with such precise lines and angles that Leia itched to grab a protractor. Only a little further and—

Leia stumbled, a sharp pain shooting through her ankle.

"Ow!" She reached for the wall, but gravity won, and she fell hard onto the packed snow floor.

It was like the ground had fallen out from under her. Now she lay aching, wondering why everything hurt so much more in her forties.

"Oh my gosh!" Kat rushed to her side. "Are you okay?" She helped Leia sit as she shifted her weight off her throbbing hip and onto her ice-cold butt. The cold penetrated her layers, her jeans soaking up melting snow.

Leia winced through gritted teeth. "I think I'm okay," she managed, even as pain shot from her ankle up her shin. She noticed a jagged hole in the sphinx's nose beside her. "Did I do that?"

The color drained from Kat's face. "Isn't the sphinx's nose supposed to be missing?"

"I swear I fell straight forward." Leia's stomach dropped. Yes, she'd instinctively reached for the wall, but she'd clearly, surely, hopefully missed and gone straight down.

"I think you tripped on this." Kat sank her boot into a soft spot in the floor.

Leia scooted over despite her screaming ankle and soaked jeans. "Strange that it's not packed hard like the rest."

"We'll tell Ian. First, let's get you back to the cabin and check that ankle."

Leia hesitated, eyeing their door. "But our room is so close." Only one door down. "Look at the curtain." It was cerulean blue. She wanted to see what was behind it.

Kat held her steady. "Can you put weight on it?"

The test step sent pain shooting up her leg. "I'll try," she said, realizing that hopping down the hall might not be the best idea.

Maybe she could crawl.

She glanced at the sphinx again. The nose was definitely odd-looking, and the shoulder showed finger marks through the carving. They could be in trouble. Her stomach churned at the thought of the damage waiver they'd signed.

"That settles it," Kat said, reading her expression. "Exit's this way. We'll have tomorrow for the room. Right now, we need to take care of that ankle. And we can talk about everything back at the cabin."

*Where no one can hear us discuss sabotage.* The words hung unspoken in Kat's worried frown.

Leia sighed. "I hate when you're right." She let Kat support her as they shuffled down the hall toward a bright red Exit sign.

She sincerely hoped she hadn't damaged the hotel before she'd even seen their room. Someone else must have done it. She hadn't felt herself touch the wall.

But their room. It had been so close.

She cast one last look at the curtained doorway as they made their way out into the crisp, cold air.

# CHAPTER EIGHT

*Tomorrow*, she vowed, leaning on her friend.

She wanted to explore their room. And more, though she wasn't exactly sure what that meant yet.

It was strange to think that after Ian and his staff ran all that heavy machinery over the graded snow floor, after they'd pulled heavy wood frames, positioned snow machines, after the artists had trampled around carving walls—one little pocket hadn't gotten compressed.

Would someone sabotage the floor? No. That was ridiculous. This place was making her paranoid.

"Tomorrow," Kat promised as Leia glanced back again.

"Tomorrow," Leia echoed, unease settling in her gut.

## CHAPTER
# NINE

Warm rays of sunlight peeked through the frost-covered window, casting a soft glow across Katherine's cozy bedroom. She burrowed deeper into her warm cocoon of blankets before reaching toward her watch on the bedside table. She found a note from Leia instead.

"Working on a surprise," she read, a smile tugging at her lips.

With any luck, it was hot cinnamon rolls. Her favorite.

Her stomach grumbled at the thought.

The smile faded as she registered the unnatural silence blanketing the cabin.

They'd stayed up ridiculously late going over everything that had happened the day before, coming to zero conclusions about anything except that someone liked to mess with other teams' equipment.

But there was one thing she'd neglected to think about last night.

She picked up the guestbook lying beneath the note and thumbed through until she found what she was looking for.

*Thanks for a cozy experience at our first 'Magic in Ice.'*
*We can't wait to come back next year!*
*Rita & Tony Marlbaugh*

A child's crooked scrawl took up too much space below: *Becca*

Year after year, the entries flowed, a stream of happy memories in looping script: *Rita, Tony, and Becca.* Later entries included hopeful notes like *We'll get 'em next year!*

The final entry hit Katherine like a punch to the gut. *Congratulations on your win, honey! We always knew you could do it. We're so proud of you and Eric. Can't wait to see you win again next year!*

The blank pages that followed spoke volumes.

Katherine tugged on her hoodie, tucked her phone into the pocket, and wandered into the living room, wishing Leia were there.

Anything to distract her from the weight of all those happy little notes.

She pulled back the window curtains. Snow-laden evergreens stretched endlessly into the distance. Heaven.

Although coffee would make it better.

At least coffee never hurt.

As she turned to brew a cup, she noticed Leia's coat was missing from its peg, and her boots were gone from the rack. At least her ankle must be feeling better. They'd iced it last night and enjoyed a bit of Bailey's-spiked cocoa.

For medicinal purposes, of course.

Katherine pulled a fresh mug from the cabinet and set the Keurig to brew a cup of Cinnabon Classic.

She'd given herself a craving.

The rich aroma of cinnamon and coffee had barely begun to fill the air when her phone buzzed in her pocket.

"Well, look at that." She found a single bar of internet connection. "A vast improvement on yesterday's zero."

Steaming mug in hand, she settled onto the couch. She'd been meaning to watch the ice hotel's information video about staying overnight. The desk clerk had said it was important, even given her a paper with the link.

Darned if she could find it now.

"Google it is." She typed *Jack Oak Resort Ice Hotel* into the search bar.

As the results loaded, Katherine's heart dropped. There, at the top of the page, sat a video of the accident that had claimed Rebecca's life.

She didn't want to see it.

She didn't want to think about it.

But after a night of dead-end theories, she couldn't ignore it.

She tapped the link before she could change her mind.

Eric's face filled the screen, a microphone thrust toward him by an eager reporter. Behind him, Rebecca worked on a sculpture in its early stages, lips pressed tight, hands moving with deliberate precision as she carved. A rough outline of a giant balance scale dominated the piece, towering at least twenty-five feet high. From it, a series of mathematical equations appeared to launch straight into the air, glittering like sparking embers.

Katherine's fingers tightened on her phone. Rebecca looked exactly like her picture in the book—same clothes, same hat, same windswept braid. Both the recording and the picture must have taken place on the day of the accident.

Eric held up his binder, the immaculate pages protected in plastic sleeves. "As you can see"—he gestured to the designs—"we have a very specific process for creating these sculptures."

The reporter leaned in with a dazzling smile. "And you figured out this process as an executive chef?"

"I had a background in engineering before the culinary world caught my attention," Eric replied. "It really helps at times like this."

*Eric Hardney, Last Year's Champion* scrolled across the bottom of the screen.

"In fact," Eric continued as excitement crept into his voice, "we're about to remove a significant piece from the right side. Our teammate Craig will demonstrate."

The camera swung to a man with amber mutton chops, clearly thrilled at his moment in the spotlight. He approached the giant, half-formed ice scale, tools clutched to his chest.

Katherine's knuckles whitened around her phone. She knew what was coming but couldn't look away.

On-screen, Craig revved his chainsaw. It seemed to be working perfectly. He raised it high. The blade's echo filled the speakers as he carved out a large section from the right side.

A chunk broke free. The sculpture swayed. For one breathless moment, everything stilled.

Then screams erupted as the entire structure crashed to the left, sending shards of ice in every direction.

The camera jerked wildly, capturing blurred flashes of falling ice and fleeing spectators before cutting to an ashen-faced news anchor.

"Well, that was certainly unexpected," he stammered, shuffling papers. "We, uh, hope everything is all right out there. Now for our high school sports report."

Seriously?

Katherine set the phone facedown, her hand trembling as her mind replayed the disaster. It had been even more terrifying than she'd imagined. Watching that sweet, smiling woman crushed under tons of ice, right in front of her family.

The door burst open, and Leia bounded in. "I just rented snowshoes!"

Katherine jumped and nearly sent her coffee flying.

Leia's grin faded. "What's wrong?"

Katherine hesitated for a moment before handing over her phone. "I was watching the accident. The one that killed Rebecca."

Leia's face fell as she watched. She returned the phone, visibly shaken. "That's...that's horrible."

"I know." Katherine's voice caught. "But Amy was right. The sculpture was stable. There were no straps or supports that could have tipped it. But what do I know about ice sculpting? Could Craig have cut it wrong? Was there something wrong with his saw?"

"The equipment seemed fine." Leia rolled her shoulders, a familiar look of determination settling over her features. She grabbed a hotel notepad and a pencil and began scribbling. "Wait. Let me see your phone." She paused the video, eyes darting between the screen and her equations.

Katherine sipped her coffee, watching her friend work.

"This doesn't make sense," Leia muttered, thrusting the notepad forward. "See?" She jabbed at a tangle of calculations.

"You're the one with the applied mathematics degree." Katherine's program had focused on dosage calculations and basic algebra. She'd cry if she had to do advanced calculus and physics and all the other crazy math classes that Leia had taken for fun. "Keep going."

Leia's eraser attacked the page. "No. Craig's cut wasn't faulty. There was more mass on his side. The sculpture should have fallen toward him." She chewed the end of the pencil before starting fresh. "I must be calculating wrong."

Katherine squeezed her friend's arm. "I'm sorry I brought it up." Leia never could let go of an unsolved problem. "Maybe there was a flaw in the ice." It didn't always come down to math. She considered herself very brave for telling Leia that.

"Maybe," Leia mumbled, brushing away the carnage from the eraser.

"No more of this," Katherine declared. "We're on vacation, and we're going to act like it."

"Where is this coming from?" Leia asked, returning pencil to paper.

"I know you. This entire vacation will become about that piece of paper." At least she had Leia's attention now. "We're not going to prove or disprove anything by watching a two-minute video on my phone."

One that thousands of people had watched before them.

"If anything, it shows that accidents do happen. Trust me." Katherine sighed. "I've missed too much in life focusing on work. Let's not turn a dream trip into an obsession."

Leia's pencil stilled, her gaze darting between Katherine and the paper.

"Maybe you're right," she conceded, adding one last number to the margin. "I just want to make things better for Trishelle and John." Her pencil ghosted over the figures. "If I could just prove whether it was an accident."

"Only we don't have all the facts."

"Stop making sense." Leia ditched her pencil. "I know I'm spinning."

"Then let's go snowshoeing and get you unspun. I can be ready in five minutes."

"Of course you can." Leia stood. "It'll take me that long to find my long underwear."

In no time at all, Leia had assembled her layers, and Katherine was changed and ready, too. Sporting a pair of abominable snowman earrings.

Leia smirked. "Nice touch."

"You too," she said, admiring the vintage-style thermometers dangling from Leia's ears.

Leia fiddled with one. "They really tell the temperature."

"Of course they do." It was Leia. "Just think." She held the door open for her friend. "We might see a moose."

"Trust me, you don't want to see a moose. Those things are terrifying."

Katherine locked the door behind them. "They're really good with sautéed mushrooms and red wine sauce with a sprinkling of minced shallots."

"Don't let them hear you say that." Leia breathed in the crisp, clear air. "If we get chased by a moose, I won't be thinking of shallots."

"I'm taking a picture," Katherine said.

She'd caption it. *Look what my crazy friend made me do.*

And she'd treasure it always.

The day was beautiful. Snow sparkled in the sunlight, a vast expanse of white stretching before them.

"All right, snowshoe time." Katherine held onto the porch rail while she strapped them to her boots. The gear wasn't strictly necessary for the immediate trail, but they'd need it for exploring off-path.

While Leia finished up, she unfolded the map from the front desk. "There's a creek-side trail to the east of the main lodge. We could loop north, past the hotel and across the parking lot to the trailhead. It'll bring us south behind the cabins on the other side of the plaza. That way, we can get our bearings before we tackle the lakeside trail." She glanced to Leia, who was double-checking her straps. "If your ankle acts up, we'll be close enough to bail and find a warm spot to park our happy butts."

"Remember, I've done this exactly twice," Leia said, standing to test the fit.

"It's not hard," Katherine said, recalling outings with her dad—sunset ventures before dinner or long hikes on blustery weekend afternoons.

For fun, she led Leia off the groomed path into the wild area behind the cabins. "It's all in the shuffle," she said, gliding onto fresh snow. "Keep a steady rhythm and you're golden."

Leia nodded, focused on mimicking Katherine's movements. After a few awkward steps, she found her pace. Soon they trekked side by side, accompanied only by crunching snow and occasional bird calls.

Leia watched a hawk soar over their heads into the forest. "I love the wilderness."

Katherine hated to burst her bubble. "We're still on the edge of the hotel parking lot. Wait until we truly get off the beaten path."

They passed the employee parking lot on the hotel's western side, navigating around resort trucks and ATVs before turning at a gate arm separating public parking from the employee access roads. Katherine felt a bit self-conscious and very, very conspicuous as they clomped across the lot, past arriving guests. But the trailhead beckoned from the eastern edge, its wooden sign peeking through fresh snow.

"This looks charming," Katherine said. "It'll take us behind the other cabins toward the lakeshore." She halted in an open spot. "Hold on, I need to adjust these straps."

Katherine squatted to sit.

"Kat, wait!" Leia's warning came too late. Katherine plopped down and immediately sank butt-first into soft powder.

"What the hey!" She flailed, snow flying everywhere.

Leia burst out laughing. "You just sat in deep powder." She moved to help. "There's a drainage ditch here. It probably runs the entire length of the parking lot."

"What ditch? It's an open field," Kat protested, struggling to get her feet under her.

"Welcome to the wonderful world of snowdrifts." Leia offered her a hand. "The wind covers many sins."

"How did you spot it?" Katherine asked, reaching up.

Leia shrugged. "Creek's right there, and there's no retention pond on the other side. Melted snow needs somewhere to go."

"I suppose," Katherine said, gripping Leia's hand.

"The parking lot slopes this way." Leia groaned with effort. "The ditch catches runoff to the creek. My driveway's similar. It keeps water from the foundation. When you get out, look for the depression under that tree."

Katherine's grip slipped, and she fell. Poof! Straight back into powder.

She attempted a rolling recovery, making things worse. "Great, now I'm sideways."

"At least it's not quicksand," Leia said, looking on the bright side.

"Ha. True." Growing up in the '80s, she'd been convinced quicksand would get her eventually.

"Let's get you up." Leia tried once again, but the more they struggled, the deeper Katherine sank, until they were both breathless from laughter.

Eventually, their thrashing compressed the snow enough for Katherine to stand and step out, giggling like a schoolgirl.

"That's one way to do it," Leia concluded.

"In hindsight," Katherine mused, "we should have gone straight to the competition area. It would have been a lot safer."

"And miss this?" Leia teased, feigning a stagger. "Never."

Katherine took her cue and staggered alongside her. "Onward!"

The trail snaked eastward, then south along the creek. The cabins vanished behind them, leaving only rustling leaves and bubbling water. Ice flows glinted in the creek. A dark-eyed junco hopped into the frigid current, splashing and preening. As they rounded a bend, the lake came into view, with the ice sculpture competition at the shoreline.

"How's your ankle holding up?" Katherine asked.

"Good. I'm going strong. Let's check on Roger's team before we hit the lakeside trail." Leia pointed to a group huddled around a large chunk of ice.

Maybe they would learn something new. Maybe they wouldn't. Katherine was just glad to be outside.

As they approached, she noticed Larry and the others had taken up Leia's suggestion from the day before. The broken pieces from the original sculpture had been arranged into an oval, with Alice and other Wonderland characters taking form on the other side.

"Hi, guys," Leia called out, waving. "Looking good!"

Larry glanced up, smiling. "Thanks to you. We know we won't win, but at least we'll have something fun to show for our efforts."

"Any sign of Roger?"

"Not yet." Larry sprayed down a piece of ice with a water gun and dunked it in the bucket. "I tried calling, but his voicemail was full."

Katherine spotted Paul nearby, his arm in a sling. Despite his injury, he was doing his best to help, handing tools to his teammates and organizing their workspace. He seemed to have a very close eye on their equipment.

She made her way over. "How's the arm, Paul?"

He shrugged, wincing. "It's been better, but I'm managing. I couldn't just sit around while my team needed me."

"Any other issues?"

"No, not at all. Didn't even see any raccoon tracks this morning. Everything around here is exactly where it should be."

Except for Roger.

Katherine nodded, glad that there were no more signs of trouble. "Just don't push yourself too hard, okay?"

Leia popped up between them. "Is that Carlos?" She pointed toward a man in a Patriot's beanie emerging from behind the looking glass.

"He's been a godsend," Paul said. "He offered to help since Amy has things under control at her camp."

"Well, that's sweet," Leia said, glancing meaningfully at Katherine.

That seemed risky, letting a member of another team into their camp after what had happened.

Katherine watched him closely. Carlos worked seamlessly with the others, skillfully shaping the ice. Maybe she'd been too quick to judge based on his prison tattoos. She was glad to see him lending a hand, giving Paul a break.

And Amy's straps had been undermined too. Carlos wouldn't have done that to his own team. Maybe he was the only one they could trust since he was a victim too.

"Ready?" Leia asked, her snowshoes pointing toward the trail.

Before Katherine could answer, a shout from Alexi's camp caught their attention. They turned to see the Russian sculptor gesturing wildly, his face red with rage, berating a young man with slim shoulders and a scruffy beard.

"*Ух ты!*" Alexi bellowed. "*Ты что, совсем идиот?*"

His teammate cowered, stuttering explanations, but Alexi was having none of it. He grabbed a nearby bucket of hot water and hurled it, narrowly missing the man. The steaming liquid hissed as it hit the snow.

Katherine stood motionless, shocked.

"What are you looking at?" Alexi demanded of his team. When his eyes met Katherine's, his demeanor changed instantly. He huffed and slapped his arms, letting out a bellowing laugh that sounded forced but practiced. "Okay, no more fooling around. We have much work still to do."

"Let's keep moving," Katherine said quietly.

"What's with him?" Leia asked as they made their way to the trailhead.

"I can't believe Alexi's temper." The dangerous anger contrasted sharply with the charming man she'd met yesterday. And how quickly he covered his slip meant he'd likely done it before. "Just goes to show that first impressions can be deceiving."

"If there is a saboteur, could it be Alexi?" Leia glanced over her shoulder.

"Why?" Katherine resisted looking back herself.

"Well, he hasn't won before. If you're sabotaging the competition, you're doing whatever it takes to win, right?"

"And then some."

"And that temper... Maybe he cares about winning a little *too* much, like Amy said."

It was possible. Then again... "We don't know if he had trouble with his straps. We didn't know to ask when we first met him."

"True," Leia conceded. "But Roger did get beat up a couple of years ago. And the way Alexi threw that bucket..."

He could have easily thrown a punch.

"Sabotage is usually a little more subtle than a punch in the face. Roger would have blamed Alexi for trying to throw the competition, and it would have been game over."

Leia pulled her hat tighter over her ears. "I'm at it again. Twisting myself in knots without enough facts."

"That's why we're out here in the snow. All Zen-like."

"We are so Zen." Leia snorted.

"Call it a goal," Katherine said, leading them into the wilds.

They followed the lakeside trail, leaving the resort behind. The path grew wilder here, a world away from manicured walkways and sculpted ice. They searched for trail markers like dark fairy-tale breadcrumbs, setting off through the pines along the frozen lake.

The sun climbed higher, warming the snowy landscape. Despite the chill, the weather was pleasant, almost balmy, without a hint of wind.

"Now this is the fantasy," Leia said, shuffling alongside her.

Katherine nodded, feeling the morning's tension dissipate. This was exactly what they'd needed, a chance to clear their heads and escape the chaos.

"Thanks for dragging me out here, Kat," Leia said, gazing out at the barren lake.

"You rented the shoes," Katherine reminded her.

Leia smiled. "Because you pointed out that this was a vacation, not another work assignment. I'm glad you're with me. Nothing could've convinced Nick to go on an adventure like this, even without the threat of moose."

"Maybe it's best that he stayed home with Charley, then. Lord help him." Katherine chuckled but caught the sadness behind her friend's words. "Is everything okay with you two?"

Leia sighed, her breath clouding. "He's great, and I love him, but ever since the kids flew the nest, Nick's just so comfortable with routine. It's getting dull, you know?" She glanced at Katherine. "My days feel like they're slipping by. One bleeds into another. A whole week can go by, and if someone asks what I've been up to, I don't remember. I've done…nothing."

Katherine nodded, understanding all too well even though for her, it was often the opposite. Too many things happening, all blurring together. An endless cycle of work and responsibility. She told herself she liked it. It kept her from thinking too hard. She hadn't realized she needed to get away until this trip. "Sometimes it's good to shake things up, to step outside your comfort zone."

"That's exactly why I'm so glad you're here. You've always been my adventure buddy."

Katherine warmed at the compliment. It had been ages

since she'd been anybody's adventure anything. "Anytime," she said automatically.

They wandered along the lake toward a distant cluster of trees that stood out from the main forest. A plow rumbled along a roadway above, its flashing yellow lights breaking the illusion of untouched wilderness. It turned a bend and disappeared, its engine fading to silence.

"I feel like I have been holed up too much lately too," Katherine admitted. "It's nice to be out in nature without being in the middle of a disaster. Part of me was beginning to see nature as the enemy. I forgot how fun it could be to just wander around in it."

"Well, I'm glad we're out here, then. Everyone needs a break sometimes."

And friends. Katherine couldn't remember the last time she'd laughed so hard at dinner. Or dragged someone out for a snowy adventure. Just the two of them.

Large snowflakes fell as clouds dimmed the sky. As they brushed the snow off their clothes, Katherine noticed an odd shape in the distance, a dark form against the white landscape. "Do you see that?" she asked, pointing toward the tree line.

Leia squinted. "Is that a moose? It's not moving."

"Not everything's a moose."

"Can't be too careful," Leia said, heading that way. "Moose are sneaky. They're like ninjas."

"Ah, yes, the elusive moose ninja." Katherine nodded. "Known for their ability to disappear behind saplings and for their devastating antler chop."

But whatever it was, it definitely wasn't an animal, Katherine realized as they drew closer. The shape was too angular, too unnaturally still. And unless moose stood around motionless for days, they didn't get that much snow piled on top of them.

Katherine's unease grew with each crunching step.

"Oh, my goodness," Leia said, pushing ahead. "It's a car."

Katherine stiffened. Leia was right.

The twisted mess of metal dead ahead was once a sleek blue sedan before its front end had wrapped around a massive evergreen. The driver's door hung open like a gaping wound.

"Hold up." Katherine took in every detail. The broken trees. The unmistakable trail of destruction softened by wind and fresh snowfall. She traced the car's path from the embankment above. "The driver must have missed the turn."

Leia halted. "I don't want to look."

"Then I'll do it," Katherine said, steeling herself.

A half-empty tequila bottle lay on the passenger seat. Crushed cigarette packs littered the floor, and the stale scent of tobacco clung to the interior.

Leia drew up behind her as Katherine ducked her head inside, noticing dark liquid pooled and frozen on the leather driver's seat.

"Oh good. It's just alcohol," Leia said.

But Katherine recognized the dark brown ice immediately. "That's not alcohol. It's blood."

Leia stumbled back. "But...where's the driver? Surely someone would have reported this."

No footprints were visible, but snow could have buried them.

Katherine examined the scene, her experience with accidents kicking in. "Why is there so much blood on the seat but none on the dash or the windshield?"

Leia had gone deathly pale. "I don't know, but we need to report this. Let's get back to the resort. Now."

Katherine nodded. She suddenly felt very alone and very vulnerable out there in the woods. Someone was in serious trouble, and the inches of snow on the car didn't bode well for finding the driver. "Let's go."

## CHAPTER
# TEN

"This seems wrong." Leia's hand hovered over a polished, lotus-blossom door handle.

It had only been a few hours since they'd found the bloody car, but it felt like an eternity.

"We did everything we could," Kat assured her.

But the words rang hollow.

They'd raced back to the hotel, legs aching, lungs burning. They'd skipped the meandering front desk line and charged straight up to the manager, their words tumbling out in a breathless rush as they described the crashed car, the blood, the deafening silence of the snow-covered forest.

They just hadn't been prepared for what came next.

"They offered us hot cocoa," Leia said.

As if that could fix it.

"And s'more cookies," Kat added, not helping.

Kat sighed, dragging a hand through her hair. "They called the police. The detective took our statements. There's a team of officers out there now because of us."

"We should be out there too," Leia insisted, itching to

do something, anything. She reached for the silly fountain on the pedestal next to the door and yanked the plug. "There." The tinkling water fell silent.

"Feel better?" Kat asked dryly.

"No."

"Sometimes the best thing to do is to step back and let the police handle it," Kat assured her.

Didn't mean Leia wanted to hear it.

"I think that's why they gave us the free spa coupons." Kat waved the glossy vouchers.

The manager had promised to keep them updated. She'd assured them that a day of relaxation would go a long way to showing the resort's appreciation for the performance of their civic duty.

"Even the door is ridiculous," Leia muttered, but it wasn't true. The spa entrance was stunning, all polished mahogany and gleaming gold, adorned with blooming flowers and swirling vines. That somehow made it worse.

They had done good, she knew that. They'd stepped up when it mattered. Maybe that was why it stung so badly to be told she wasn't needed anymore.

"Let's just try it." Kat slipped past her to push the door open. The scent of lavender and vanilla drifted out. "If it's torture, we can leave."

A friendly spa employee checked them in and led them to the relaxation grotto, which was even more ridiculous than the name. Leia lingered at the door, adjusting to the soft lighting and artfully placed flameless candles. Plush loungers lined up in front of the soothing trickle of water from the rock wall fountain.

She couldn't get away from the fountains.

Kat made her way to one of the loungers. "If we don't use the vouchers while we're here, they'll go to waste."

"You're hitting below the belt, appealing to my inner cheapskate." Leia followed along. "You know I don't like wasting things."

"Whatever it takes," Katherine said, settling in. "This morning was intense. I, for one, am glad we could grab a snack and then try to calm down here, where we apparently have more snacks." She leaned back as a young woman in a Serenity Spa polo shirt set a plate of fruit and cheese on the small table between them.

Leia tried to focus on the warm earthy tones of the decor and the potted evergreens dotting the space, but her mind kept circling back. "It has to be Roger's car," she said, her voice breaking through the forest soundtrack. "How many people are driving around with Manitoba plates? Plus that car had a few days' worth of snow built up on the top. That means he's been out in subzero temperatures since Tuesday night. There's no way he's still alive out there."

Kat adjusted her robe. "We don't know anything for sure. We didn't see any ID in the car."

"True, but Roger's the only one not around to report," Leia pointed out.

Kat tapped her fingers against the arms of her chair, thinking. "Even if it was Roger who was hurt, he might have stumbled away from the accident and made it to a hospital. They wouldn't necessarily contact anyone here about it since no one here is family."

Leia crossed, then uncrossed her legs. "But the police would have found and removed the car if Roger reported the accident." She leaned closer. "What if he didn't make it to a hospital? If he was drunk and wandered off, he could be lying dead under a tree or trapped in a snowdrift somewhere on that frozen lake. All alone."

"That would be terrible," Kat said softly.

"We should have looked harder." Done more.

Kat shook her head. "Wandering any farther off the marked trail could have gotten us lost. It's way too easy to get turned around out there." She drew her shoulders back. "Besides, we did exactly what we needed to do. We found the car, reported it, and our tracks will lead the police straight there. That's more than anyone did before today." At Leia's restless look, she added, "We also made it back safely without adding two more missing people to the police docket."

She was right.

Leia *knew* she was right.

But that didn't stop her from rapping her foot against the carpet like a woodpecker drilling into a tree.

Yes, they'd handled the situation this morning, but she somehow wanted to handle it more. "I don't get how you can just turn it off."

"I'm not," Kat admitted, halting her own bouncing foot. "I always want to help. I made it my job." She ran a hand through her hair. "But when I've done what I can, I have to let it go, or it will drive me crazy."

"Good point," Leia said, because she was going a bit stir-crazy.

The spa attendant returned with two glasses of prosecco. "Is there something wrong with the food?" she asked, eyeing their untouched snacks.

"No, it's great," Leia said quickly.

"We just had a morning." Kat reached for the sparkling wine.

"Did you ever," said a platinum blonde from the last chair by the door. How long had she been there? "Another prosecco and a hummus plate, please," she said to the attendant before the girl scurried off.

The woman strutted down the row and took the chair beside Leia. "So, you found Roger Cullins's car crashed into a tree?" she asked baldly, not even bothering to hide her interest.

"We did," Leia said before Kat could deny it. "We went out snowshoeing and found a wrecked car by the lake. The whole thing reeked of tequila and cigarettes, and there was blood on the seat."

The woman's perfectly manicured hand flew to her mouth.

"That's the opposite of letting it go," Kat reminded her.

"That's awful," the woman exhaled. "Roger Cullins was last year's winner, right?"

"The Ice King himself," Leia said. "Hi, by the way. I'm Leia," she said as the woman took a sip, "and this is my friend Kat. Um, Katherine."

"Caitlyn Wu," the blonde said, lifting her glass in a mock toast.

"Are you related to Amy Wu?" Kat asked, selecting a piece of cheese.

Caitlyn brightened. "She's my big sis."

Fun. "So you're staying in the ice hotel tonight?" Leia asked.

Caitlyn barked out a laugh. "Absolutely not." She gave a mock shiver. "I, like a delicate flower, wilt in the cold." She took a sip of her wine. "I come up every year to support Amy. But I spend twenty minutes outside, tops, for the award ceremony." She smoothed back a lock of hair. "In the meantime, I am keeping my happy butt right here for the rest of the weekend."

"That's a fantastic goal," Leia agreed as the attendant returned with Caitlyn's plate. Suddenly, the food looked better, the spa felt plusher. Leia eased her shoulders back, reaching for a grape. "How do you think Amy is going to do this year?"

"Well, she's my sister, so I think she should win every year," Caitlyn said, dipping a toasted pita in hummus. "But seriously, I think her prospects are excellent. She's been working on her designs since last May, and I absolutely love the mermaids and sea serpent she came up with. Talk about stunning."

Leia split a wedge of cheese with Kat. "It was shaping up great the last time we saw it."

Caitlyn nodded. "And now that Carlos is on the team, they'll really come to life. He's one of the most talented artists I've seen."

"We saw him working on the dragon sculpture in the main lobby," Kat said. "He was a bit gruff."

Caitlyn laughed. "Yeah, that's Carlos." She retrieved her wine. "Normally Amy has terrible taste in men, but Carlos is an okay guy so far. At least to her," she added with a tip of her glass. As if that made it okay. She took a sip, then motioned to the attendant for another glass. "He's certainly better than Amy's last boyfriend. He messed her up."

"We've all had one like that," Leia said, popping the grape into her mouth.

Caitlyn lifted her glass in a silent salute. "I don't understand how she got so wrapped up. He was too old for her. She fell for him in five seconds flat. Then—boom. It was over. It blew my mind how devastated she was."

Kat traced the rim of her glass. "I think a lot of us have been there."

"Oh, I know it's not always the length. It's the intensity." Caitlyn took a healthy sip. "I guess that's why it bugs me so much. He should have been nothing more than a blip on the romance radar. Typical Amy, getting in too deep. She kept calling him Red like she was starring on a knockoff of *Sex and the City*. It was weird." She selected another slice of pita. "Anyhow, he was a user and a cheat, and she didn't leave her apartment for two months straight after they broke up." She shook her head. "I'd like to kick that guy in the nuts, but to this day, Amy refuses to tell me his real name."

"Maybe she'd like to forget," Leia suggested.

"I hope so," Caitlyn said, trading in her empty glass for a fresh one. "I'm just glad Amy's doing better now."

"With Carlos?" Kat asked pointedly. "It seems he has a past as well."

Leia shot her friend a look.

"Amy deserves to know," Kat pressed.

Caitlyn's shoulders tensed. "About Carlos doing time? She knows. I was the one who swore not to tell Mom and Dad." She dipped another pita, her movements sharp. "Amy says it was just a dumb mistake, that he was young and didn't have access to a decent attorney."

She took a bite. "Anyway, according to her, he's done his time and turned over a new leaf." She waved a hand dismissively. "In any case, I think she's in it for the long haul this time, finally. They have plans to open an urban art studio in Boston. They're hoping if they can win this year, it will help get the studio off the ground."

"Amy's talent is amazing," Leia said, recalling the lifelike detail she'd seen, even in the unfinished piece. "It can't be easy being a woman in the competition."

Caitlyn wedged an elbow on her armrest. "Amy could tell you stories that would curl your hair." She pressed her lips together. "It's sad that Amy and Rebecca didn't get along when they met. They could have formed a girls' squad to take on the boys."

"Oh, I'd pay to see that," Kat said.

"Rebecca could have been an excellent mentor," Caitlyn mused. "They probably would have had the competition in the bag for years, seeing as Rebecca was the real talent behind the Hardney team."

Wait. "Why do you say that?" Leia asked.

"Easy." Caitlyn eased back in her chair. "That team hasn't won since they lost Rebecca." She waved the thought away. "I don't bring it up anymore. It ruined our first year here. Amy doesn't like to talk about the accident or Rebecca. Ever."

That was a little dramatic.

Kat popped a grape into her mouth. "Has Amy ever won the competition?"

It sounded like a casual question.

Leia knew it wasn't.

Caitlyn's face clouded. "We thought they had it in the bag the year before last." Her fingers traced the rim of her glass. "But something threw Amy off. She didn't even finish on time."

Leia cocked her head. "That doesn't seem like her from what you've told us."

"Exactly." Caitlyn's lips pressed together in a thin line. "She might look like a free-spirit artsy type, but she's type A all the way and extremely competitive. I have no idea what happened, and naturally, she doesn't want to talk about that, either." She winced. "Their team got disqualified for not finishing a required element. Amy was heartbroken."

Interesting. "Is that why Carlos bristles every time Roger gets mentioned? Because he won that year?"

Caitlyn thought for a moment. "I have no idea. I asked Carlos what was going on, but he only said to look at Roger's room and I would know."

"So?" Kat pressed.

"You didn't go and look?" Leia finished.

Caitlyn appeared a bit taken aback. "I would have had to go tromping through the ice box. Besides, I don't know what Roger's room is supposed to look like."

"I'd have been curious," Leia said.

Caitlyn waved her off. "I was only here one day that year, and I wasn't about to get mixed up in artist drama. Anyway, it doesn't matter now. Amy's going to win this year. I'm sure of it."

The spa attendant returned. "Miss Wu, we're ready for your Nordic salt scrub."

Caitlyn rose from her chair with fluid grace. "Well, duty calls. I'll see you at the awards ceremony when Amy holds up that enormous check." With a turn worthy of a model on a runway, she followed the attendant out.

Leia sank deeper into her plush lounger. "Well, that's interesting. I didn't think we'd be getting tea with our prosecco."

Kat's gaze drifted to the door. "What Caitlyn said about Amy getting so thrown off she didn't finish. That's weird."

"I know, right?" If Roger got drunk and wrapped his car around a tree in the snow, that could have been an accident. And after seeing the video of the sculpture collapse, that certainly could have been an accident, too. Leia's data column for random terrible luck looked pretty solid in spite of the still unsolved math problem on the coffee table in the cabin.

But someone beating Roger up was not an accident.

Neither was what had happened to Paul. "Do you think Amy was sabotaged? She was on track to win, and then what? What happened that she won't tell her sister about?"

"To be fair, her sister likes to talk," Kat said, sipping her wine.

"Okay, true. But she's here supporting her." Leia leaned forward. "And Carlos thinks Roger had something to do with it."

"But Roger's camp was attacked *this* year. And how would he have sabotaged her by carving art in his own room?" Kat nibbled on a piece of cheese, thinking. "That doesn't make sense. And only Carlos knows what happened."

"Not just Carlos," Leia said, crossing her arms.

"What do you mean?"

"Carlos told Caitlyn to check Roger's room that year if she wanted to know what was wrong with Amy. Caitlyn didn't take him seriously. She didn't even look."

Kat sat up. "But Trishelle would have! And she'd have taken pictures!"

The attendant slipped into the room, a serene smile on her lips. "Are you ready for your treatments, ladies?"

"Not anymore," Leia said as the implications of what Kat had said unfolded.

Caitlyn might not have wanted to hunt down the clue Roger left. Heck, she might not have known what she was looking at if she did. But Leia wouldn't pass up a chance like that.

"Trishelle and John signed up for cross-country skiing today," Kat said, slipping out of her chair. "She mentioned it last night."

"Then we'll ask them when they get back," Leia vowed.

## CHAPTER TEN

"And relax in the meantime," Kat said, tightening her robe. "Vacation, remember?"

"Gotcha." Yes, they were here for a reason. "We're here to smell the roses and all that."

This. Was. A. Vacation.

But it seemed a whole lot of mystery had decided to come with it.

## CHAPTER
# ELEVEN

The spa door burst open, and Katherine and Leia charged out, wobbling the meditating Buddha statue on the table next to the door.

"So much for serenity," Katherine said, sidestepping a lotus in bloom. Leia was on the hunt now, and if she knew her friend, she wouldn't stop until she had answers.

Leia flashed a grin. "Who needs cucumber slices when we've got a mystery to solve?"

*Fair enough.* They made a beeline for the elevators. Katherine jabbed the button while Leia took a second to replug the serenity fountain she'd killed.

"It's the little things," she said, joining Katherine in the elevator.

They'd start with the little things.

Like finding their friend.

Katherine checked her watch. "Trishelle is probably at dinner," she said as the elevator dinged and deposited them in the lobby.

The Lumberjack's Lodge restaurant overlooked the tree line at the back of the resort. They blazed past the hostess stand and weaved their way through the tables, scanning for their friends.

"No sign of them," Leia said after they'd made a full circuit of the room.

Katherine's stomach grumbled. "Maybe we should grab a quick bite while we're here."

"Like a stakeout," Leia said, eyes brightening.

They snagged a table near the window and ordered a couple of burgers. Katherine kept an eye on the door while they waited. Their friends would be famished after a day of cross-country skiing, and it wasn't as if they'd be downing popcorn in their cabin. "Where else could they be?"

Leia checked the door. Again. "Maybe back at the cabins already. It's getting late."

They wolfed down their burgers as soon as the food arrived, then bundled up and headed out into the cold. Flaming torches lit the path to the cabins nestled among the pines.

But when they reached Trishelle and John's cabin, the windows lay dark. Katherine rapped on the door anyhow, hoping against hope, but there was no answer.

"Frickety-frick," Leia muttered, shoving her hands into her pockets.

Katherine's attention drifted to the stream of people flowing down the torchlit path toward the ice hotel. "The competition must be wrapping up."

Trishelle wouldn't miss that.

"Let's go." Leia was already moving.

The crowd thickened near the lakeshore. Excitement buzzed in the air, and snippets of conversation drifted past.

"...the most detailed sculpture I've ever seen..."

"...can't believe they pulled it off in time."

"...heard there was an accident."

## CHAPTER ELEVEN

Katherine and Leia exchanged a glance at that last one but kept pushing forward, past towering evergreens dripping with twinkling lights, past crackling bonfires and the s'mores stand, where marshmallow-chocolate scents mixed with the crisp winter air.

"Wait. Stop." Katherine halted near a trio of snowmen. "We'll need to be careful asking about Roger's room. And Amy. We're outsiders here. If we push too hard, people will shut down."

She remembered being on the other side, kids prying about her own tragedy.

"You know I'm always on your side," Leia said without a scrap of hesitation.

"I know." The certainty in Leia's tone caught Katherine off guard. "I just don't want to be that person, pushing where it hurts."

"I know," Leia said. "We'll be the picture of tact."

As they neared the hot cocoa station, Katherine spotted a familiar couple. "Mark! Lisa!"

"My favorite newbies!" Mark closed the distance between them. "Can you believe it's almost over?"

"It's been quite a ride," Leia said. "Have you seen Trishelle by any chance?"

"No. Sorry," Lisa said. "We just got here ourselves."

Katherine scanned the packed crowd. Voices rose as spectators shuffled forward, necks craning toward the competition area. A man bounced on his toes near the front. Katherine checked her watch. Any minute now, the air horn would signal the rush to view the finished sculptures.

John trotted up, waving a paper. "Greetings, all! Guess what I get to do?"

"Don't tell me you're taking bets," Mark teased.

"I'm this year's Lord of the Drink," the physician

announced. "In charge of mirth, mayhem, and celebratory hot cocoa."

"A vital task," Katherine said.

John flashed his flask. "Don't I know it?"

"They picked the right guy," Leia said.

John tucked the flask away, shivering against the cold. "Eric wrote down everyone's order." He placed the list on the counter.

"Where's Trishelle while you carry out your sacred duty?" Leia asked.

"Down early for the final competition shots. You know her," he said, accepting a hot chocolate for himself. "She has to capture every moment."

"We're counting on it," Katherine said.

The girl behind the counter set John's hot cocoa box down just as Paul approached with a faded five-gallon bucket. "Can I get a hot water fill?"

"Always," the girl chirped.

Paul retrieved John's list as a gust of wind blew it across the counter. He glanced at it before handing it back to John. "Hey, is Roger back?" he asked, eyeing the box of hot cocoas as John added a generous splash from the flask that would make a bootlegger proud. "Have you seen him?"

"No," Leia jumped in. "Actually, we found a car wrecked in the woods today. We're afraid it might be his."

Leia would never be called subtle. But now that they were in it...

"It doesn't look good," Katherine dove in, instantly regretting her words. She took a deep breath, wishing they could start over, that she could somehow soften the blow. "Did he drive a blue sedan with Manitoba plates?"

"FMR 763?" Leia added.

Paul froze, his face blank. "Yes, that's his." His voice

came out mechanical as he looked past them toward the tree line. "You actually found his car?"

"I'm so sorry," Leia said, watching Paul drag a hand down his face.

He waved her off, hastily swiping at his eyes. "I guess it was only a matter of time."

Katherine hesitated before asking, "What do you mean?"

Paul looked down, shoving his hands into his pockets. "Roger was a drinker," he said quietly. "Drove our team crazy. Around ten each night, even during work, he'd take off. Said he wouldn't go far, but..." He shook his head. "There's this dive bar we all like up around the bend. He always ended up there. The next morning, he'd be useless. I mean, once or twice, sure, but all the time?"

"There was an open tequila bottle in the car," Katherine said. "The driver's door was open, and no one was inside." She held back mentioning the blood.

Paul ran a hand over the back of his neck. "That's odd. Roger wasn't a tequila guy. Not since a bad night in college, or so he said. Whiskey was his poison." His eyes went distant. "I hope he walked away from that crash."

Katherine's stomach knotted at the thought of Roger wandering drunk and injured into the frozen woods. By the look on Paul's face, it was clear he didn't think Roger's survival was likely either. "Did he always go out alone?" she asked, hoping against hope he'd grabbed a friend for the ride.

Paul scrubbed at his beard. "Alexi used to join him, especially early on during construction. If his work was done." He gestured weakly. "But it's been a while. And Alexi never needed it like Roger did. I don't remember Alexi coming by our camp at all for the last couple of years."

The server leaned out the hot cocoa window. "Your water's ready, but it's heavy."

Mark followed Paul through the side door to help with the bucket.

Paul gripped the handle with his good hand, nodding his thanks. "I should head back." He checked his watch, then waved his casted arm. "Take care."

"We'll make sure you've got it," Mark said, trailing after Paul with Lisa in his wake.

Once they were out of earshot, Leia turned to John and Katherine. "Could Roger have gone drinking that night and driven off the road?"

John frowned. "Unlikely. Tuesday night was the competition kick-off party. Free drinks at the hotel. Why would Roger go pay at a dive bar?"

"Was he definitely at the party?" Katherine asked.

"I talked to him," John said. "He kept hinting at his competition ideas, trying to get me to guess. He thought my Flying Purple People Eater idea had merit. Even bought me a drink for it."

"But the drinks were free," Leia said.

"Which tells you exactly what he thought of my idea."

"So he was definitely there," Katherine said.

"At least for a while," Leia added. "When did he leave?"

John thought for a moment. "He walked out right when Alexi started singing karaoke, which in retrospect was a fantastic idea."

"Why?" Katherine asked.

"He always sings 'Ice Ice Baby.'" John cringed. "And he still doesn't know all the words. But Roger seemed sober when he left. Alexi, though, he'd definitely had a few." He grinned despite himself. "He'd mixed up this ridiculously large batch of a drink his mother used to make. It tasted like fruit compote and packed enough vodka to knock out a bear."

Leia chuckled.

"I like a strong drink, but that stuff made my hair fall out." John whipped off his stocking cap, rubbing his bald head.

"Excuses, excuses," Leia mused.

"Did anyone leave with Roger?" Katherine pressed. She knew she was pushing it, but with Leia keeping things light, she could push harder.

They were actually a pretty good team.

John considered the question. "People were in and out all night. Carlos didn't stay long. I don't think Eric showed up at all."

The air horn blared. The crowd erupted.

It was time.

"You'd better go," John said, arranging his doctored cocoas.

Leia hesitated. "As long as you don't need help carrying anything."

John waved her off. "I'm a doctor. Steady hands are part of the job."

Katherine had already started walking.

"Is this situation going to get any more complex?" Katherine asked once Leia caught up.

"Yes, but WWHPD?"

"Say what?" Katherine scooped up an abandoned hot cocoa cup and tossed it in a bin.

Leia looked over her shoulder, her chin lowered. "What Would Hercule Poirot Do?"

Katherine barked out a laugh despite herself. "You're quoting my mystery novels back at me?"

"Got your attention, didn't I? Think about it. If you're

only looking at the evidence like Hercule Poirot would, you have to consider the crash an accident."

She was right. "I hate when you make sense."

"Me too. But we saw no foul play, and John didn't notice anything wrong at the party."

They dodged a family of four hauling a sled with a dog. And snacks.

That was brave.

"Someone was after him though. His camp was sabotaged." Katherine lowered her voice. "What if someone slipped him something?"

"But why?" Leia pressed. "The competition hadn't even started. He'd have plenty of time to recover."

"True. What wouldn't he recover from?"

"Stolen or altered plans," Leia suggested. "You can replace tools. We saw extras in the workshop. But lose your road map?" She slashed a hand under her throat. "That project is toast."

Katherine lowered her voice as a couple walked by. "Roger wasn't drunk at the party, but the car crash looked like drunk driving. And from the angle his car went over the ridge, he was heading to the bar, not coming back." She spun to face Leia, walking backward. "What if someone slipped him something? They could've gotten his plans, shown their whole team. Maybe even altered them to make his sculpture unstable. He wouldn't remember any of it."

"And then Roger, drugged and confused, goes on autopilot." Leia steered them toward the flaming torches, away from the crowd. "Like Trishelle walking to our cabin without thinking. He gets in the car, believing he needs to drive home."

"Takes the wrong turn at the bend." Katherine's stomach dropped. "And crashes."

Leia stopped, torchlight flickering across her face. "If the saboteur isn't just messing with tools, if they're tampering with plans too—maybe that's what happened to Rebecca. Someone could have altered the Hardney team's calculations."

Katherine exhaled slowly. That would explain why Leia couldn't spot what went wrong—the numbers were bad from the start. "Roger always wins. He'd be the perfect target."

Leia nodded. "We should look into that."

A chill ran down Katherine's spine. "If Roger was drugged, he couldn't have survived that crash."

Which meant if there was a saboteur, they were dealing with a murderer.

"We need proof," Leia said, starting to walk again. "We should check the sculptures, see if other teams have had problems with their calculations. And find out why Carlos told Caitlyn to look at Roger's room a couple of years ago. Which means talking Trishelle into showing off her pictures."

"That won't be hard." Katherine tossed a playful elbow at her friend.

But as they merged into the crowd flowing down to the lakeshore, she knew finding Trishelle would be.

## CHAPTER
# TWELVE

The crowd swept toward the lakeshore, pulling Leia and Kat along.

"This feels like those metal band concerts from college," Leia shouted over the excited chatter. "Remember the mosh pit?"

Kat sidestepped a particularly enthusiastic group. "I was too busy sneaking up to the VIP suites."

Her loss.

And Leia's gain when Katherine had returned with airline bottles of booze.

The crowd finally spread out near the competition area, and Leia felt her heart speed up. The massive sculptures loomed ahead, transformed by a dance of colored lights—greens bleeding into blues, purples melting into reds, all of it shimmering across the ice.

Leia steered them toward the closest display. "Let's start here."

Kat craned her neck. "Did you see Trishelle?"

"Not yet." She scanned the sea of faces. There was no telling where they'd find their new friend. In the meantime, the first display was the least crowded. Despite her youthful mosh-pit days, Leia preferred a bit of elbow room.

They stopped at the base of a towering Pegasus lit from the inside with gold.

Kat stopped dead. "It's like they knew I watched *Clash of the Titans* 812 times as a kid."

"You just liked Harry Hamlin with his shirt off."

"He made me feel funny. Good funny," Kat said with a dreamy sigh.

"That's why we let you pop it in the VCR 812 times."

Harry Hamlin or not—and in this case, unfortunately not—the team had done an impressive job capturing the illusion of wind in the creature's mane and tail.

"But look," Leia said, "all four hooves are on the ground."

"And the wings are stacked straight up from the back. They look more like dragon scales than feathers." Kat rubbed her chin. "I don't think this team felt confident enough to place those wings at a more natural angle."

Kat was right.

It was still a valiant effort. Probably from a younger, less-experienced team.

A group of excited twenty-somethings in matching blue and white polka dot beanies bounced up to the sculpture, phones out for selfies. They took turns posing with their creation, their laughter and chatter filling the air.

"Let's keep moving," Leia murmured.

Kat was already three steps ahead, when—

"Excuse me!" A blonde with pigtails poking out of her team beanie called to Leia, her face flushed with excitement. "Could you take a picture of all of us?"

"Sure." Leia took the camera and waited while the team lined up, their good cheer infectious. The Pegasus was

## CHAPTER TWELVE

impressive. She certainly couldn't carve a flying horse from ice. But it wasn't polished enough to place. It wasn't gravity-defying or dangerous.

"You can't keep all four legs on the ground and expect to win," Kat said after they'd moved on.

"True. But look at how happy they are. It's not about winning for them." Leia smiled at the thought. "I don't think those kids have anything to do with sabotage."

"Me either."

Around them, the competition grounds buzzed with energy. Spectators clutched hot beverages, their breath forming tiny clouds in the crisp air. Laughter and occasional bursts of applause echoed as people discovered particularly impressive sculptures.

"Come on," Leia said. "Let's see what other masterpieces we can find. Maybe spot some clues along the way."

"You two! Over here!" Larry waved them over. "Prepare to be amazed."

And they were. Before them stood a life-sized Alice in Wonderland, her icy form poised mid-step as she reached through the frame of a broken mirror. Her curiosity radiated through the glittering statue as she ventured through the oval opening formed from the broken remnants of the team's original ice sculpture. It was even better than Leia had imagined. Alice felt alive and in motion, and the team had transformed the jagged edges into a true wonderland, with lace-like flowers and mushrooms making the imperfections appear intentional. Whimsical.

Perfect.

On the opposite side, a purple-lit Cheshire Cat perched atop a mushroom. Behind it, a smoking Caterpillar and a Dodo dressed like a naval officer completed the scene. The icy smoke rising from the Caterpillar's pipe looked wispy and dreamlike. Leia let out a low whistle.

"Larry, this is genius." The ice really did look like smoke.

He drank in her praise. "Thanks, Leia. We worked hard on it."

"Did you see the whiskers on the Cheshire Cat?" Kat's voice floated from behind the looking glass. "They're so delicate."

Each whisker was a gossamer thread, barely visible yet undeniably there. "I can't believe you pulled this off after everything that happened."

Larry's smile faltered. "Paul told us about the car you found. We're all hoping for the best, but..." He trailed off.

Leia wished she could give him a hug. "We're so sorry, Larry. But there's always hope."

"He'd be proud of what you've accomplished here," Kat said, joining them.

Larry's lips twisted ruefully. "Roger did a lot of things he probably shouldn't be proud of in this competition, but if he had been on this job, there'd be a Jabberwocky flying through the air, defying the laws of physics."

"Well, I love the Dodo," Leia said, filing away his comment for later. "Even if he's respectfully on the ground."

"Dodos aren't known for their flying ability," Kat said. "As a fan of realism, I think you nailed it."

"Agreed." Leia smiled as she checked the time on the white rabbit's watch. "Roger might have defied physics, but you didn't defy literature. If you want to get technical, the Jabberwock isn't even in the book. It's only in the title. Hollywood invented the actual 'Jabberwocky.'"

Larry chuckled at that.

"I hope you continue to lead the team in the future."

# CHAPTER TWELVE

When Larry squinched his face, Leia doubled down. "I mean it. I have no doubt you can handle anything else you set your mind to."

He'd done remarkably well despite the collapse of their sculpture and the disappearance, and likely death, of his friend.

"I think I need you cheering me on all the time," Larry said.

Paul approached with a bottle of Scotch and a bittersweet smile. "I think it's time we raised a glass to our fallen comrade." He unscrewed the cap as the rest of the team gathered.

A girl in a pink stocking cap produced a set of red Solo cups. They passed the stack, and Paul poured generous servings.

"To Roger," Paul began, best-man style. "The only dickwad Canadian I've ever met. For that, we salute you."

"Hear, hear!" The team raised their cups.

The woman in the pink toque spoke next. "Rog, you were living proof God has a sense of humor. He gave you the personality of a rabid wolverine and the hands of an artist. We'll miss you, you cranky son of a bitch."

Larry guffawed.

The tributes continued, each more colorful than the last.

"To Roger, who could freeze hell over with his attitude and then carve it into a masterpiece. You were one of a kind, you miserable old jackass."

"Roger, you had the charm of a rattlesnake and the tact of a bulldozer. But when it came to sculpting, you were Michelangelo. Here's to you, you insufferable genius."

"To Roger, the only man who could piss off a saint and

still have them admiring his work. You may have been a jerk, but you were our jerk. Rest easy, buddy."

Larry stepped forward. "Rog, we'd carve next year's sculpture to look like you, but I don't think they'd like us to do an asshole."

"You could put a light in it!" somebody yelled, sparking another round of raucous laughter and toasts. "And give it a cigarette."

As the team fell into reminiscing, Leia and Kat slipped away.

"I would have liked to have met Roger," Leia mused.

"From the sound of it, you'd have had your hands full."

True. Still, meeting him would've been the only way to get a straight read—genius or toxic jerk? Maybe both. The roast felt cathartic, but their relief was palpable.

"Oh, Alexi," Leia murmured as they approached the next camp.

The Slavic goddesses were spectacular. Beautiful and terrifying, the icy figures battled under the shimmering lights. The goddess of winter raised her sickle high, leaving an arching trail of snowflakes. Their dresses froze in waves so realistic Leia almost expected them to ripple in the wind.

Kat stood beside her. "It's incredible. The movement. The detail."

"Alexi has to be a real contender this year." The only flaw was a collection of odd lines where the ice seams met, giving parts of the statue an unfinished look. Still, it was a mesmerizing display.

Right on cue, the artist emerged from behind his creation, an Igloo jug under one arm, Dixie cups swinging from the other. He spotted them and swaggered over.

"Ladies!" He spread his arms wide. "Welcome to the ultimate battle! You like?"

"More like love," Leia said.

"Congratulations, Alexi," Kat piped in. "Your sculpture is absolutely stunning."

Alexi puffed with pride and gave a slight bow. "I'll let you in on a little secret." He dodged a trio of ladies to join them. "This is my best one yet. Even I'm surprised at how it turned out."

"Interesting," Kat said. "So it came out exactly as planned?"

"Yes and no." His forehead squinched. "You can have a design." He gestured with his hands, the Igloo jug sloshing precariously. "You can know everything about how you want it to go. But after that, it's just you and the ice, and sometimes it just goes beyond anything you thought you imagined."

Leia clasped her gloved hands together. "I'm so happy for you."

"Join me in a toast?" he asked, hefting the jug under his arm.

"Er…I'm not a big drinker," Leia hedged. And not just because it lacked crushed candy canes. She and Kat needed to stay sharp.

And find Trishelle.

Alexi poured her a cup anyway, the crimson concoction turning the clear cup as bright as the ones in Roger's camp. "Trishelle says you like the sweet drinks. You will like this."

Her new friend needed to learn when to stop talking.

Kat accepted the second glass. "Have you seen Trishelle?"

"She was here and gone." Alexi poured himself one and raised it high. The aroma of fruity liquor wafted through the air.

They clinked cups, and Leia sipped, the fiery alcohol

sending a rush of warmth through her. She tasted berries and cinnamon and—

"What's in this?" Kat took a heartier second sip.

Alexi pressed his lips together, pleased. "It's my mother's recipe. Packs a punch, no?"

Leia nodded, the drink already going straight to her head. "It's delicious. Dangerous, too, I think."

"It's mother's milk to me," Alexi said, taking a large swig.

"You're a good son to give all this up for her." It was sad to think this would be his last big competition.

He locked eyes with her, studying her like one of his ice blocks. "Mama is my heart." He thumped his chest, voice thick. "She knows my soul. No one can love me like her."

Leia touched a hand to her own heart.

Kat observed and sipped.

"We just came from Roger's camp," Leia said. "They're toasting him like he's gone. I hope everyone's wrong and that he's okay."

Alexi's cheeks reddened, his spine stiffening.

"I'm so sorry," Leia rushed to continue. "I shouldn't have brought it up. I heard you two were friends."

"Friends?" Alexi spat. "A real friend would never use Mama against me." His cup crackled in his grip. "He is dead to me."

"I—" Leia began.

But Alexi slammed his cup down and stomped off, leaving them in stunned silence.

She looked to Kat. "That was—"

"Abrupt," Kat finished, watching red bleed into the snow.

"I was going to say passionate," Leia offered weakly. But what did he mean about Roger using his mother?

They started walking.

"Everyone's really on edge," Kat said under her breath. "Larry's team with the doom toasts. Alexi's fit just now."

"Right, but I don't see equipment issues or problems with Alexi's plans. Things went well. Which is automatically suspicious."

"My thoughts exactly."

Just then, Lisa came barreling down on them, with Mark hot on her heels. "You all *have* to see this!"

Mark motioned them toward a bustling camp while Lisa parted the crowd. Leia followed unsteadily, that compote drink still warming her veins.

She stumbled to a stop. Before her stood Icarus, his body twisted and tumbling in a breathtaking display of movement and light.

The glowing orange-yellow sun cast an ethereal backlight, creating the illusion of falling through the sky.

"He planned the sun into his design." Leia circled it, transfixed. "It feels like it's moving with me."

"Look at the feathers," Kat whispered. "The crosshatched cuts make them appear so light."

Yet full of texture.

A single hand and one wingtip grazed the ground at the narrow base. Every curve and angle conveyed desperate beauty, and the craftsmanship was unmatched.

"There's no way this doesn't win," Mark said. "It literally defies gravity."

"I think we might be looking at the next Ice King," Kat said.

"Try Ice Emperor." Leia would crown him herself.

"Did I hear my name?" Eric asked, offering Mark a jovial high five.

"For the first time in my life," Leia began, clearing her throat, "I may be speechless."

Eric endured their praise until he held up a hand. "Enough. Or my head won't fit through the door."

The moment of levity was short-lived. "Listen," Eric said, sobering quickly, "I heard you found Roger's car by the lake."

"We did," Kat said carefully, eyes flicking to Leia. "It's a shame."

Eric nodded slowly. He opened his mouth, closed it, then tried again. "Don't count him out," he said finally. "Roger's wily. I half expect him to come sneaking up behind me."

Leia appreciated his optimism. "Really?"

"He's tough, with a good head on his shoulders." Eric huffed out a breath. "He'll probably say he disappeared so I could win for once."

Mark laughed. "He does like to make fun of your binder."

Eric held up his hands in mock surrender. "Sue me if I laminate my plans." He hitched a shoulder. "Worked out, didn't it?"

Leia wasn't about to argue with results. And yet, this was another camp without any equipment problems, and Eric had his plans safe in his binder. "By the way, have you seen Trishelle?"

"She and John were looking at Amy's entry," Mark said.

Leia followed his gaze. "We'd best catch up."

They weaved through the crowd toward Amy's camp. A resounding *pop* pierced the air, followed by a shout. Amy stood on a crate, backlit by a floodlight, champagne foaming over her fingers.

"Looks like they've got reason to celebrate," Leia said, taking in their final sculpture.

The mermaids and sea serpent were otherworldly, scales shimmering under twinkling lights. The mermaids' hair billowed in an invisible current, while the serpent coiled around them, jaws frozen in a silent roar. Brilliant connections held the mermaids aloft, creating the illusion of weightlessness. Though it lacked the motion of Eric's sculpture, it defied gravity in its own way.

Amy's team gathered at the base, flushed with excitement. Carlos raised a bottle of O'Doul's, and for the first time, Leia understood what Amy saw in him.

When he was unguarded, open—he looked like a different person.

"Congratulations, Amy." Kat wove her way toward the artist, who was now drinking straight from the bottle. "It looks stellar."

"We didn't have a single setback once we got the ice stacked safely." Amy wiped her mouth on her coat sleeve. "Can you believe it?"

She leapt down to greet more well-wishers.

Leia approached Carlos. "Hey, you were great helping Larry's team. Both sculptures turned out amazing, and I loved the details in your ice room, too."

Carlos ducked his head, smiling bashfully. "Thank you, Leia. That means a lot."

Kat joined them. "We met Caitlyn earlier," she said, her voice casual. Too casual. "Amy's sister is impressed with you, but she mentioned something about an incident in Roger's room throwing Amy off a couple of years ago."

Carlos stiffened, his smile vanishing in an instant.

A humorless huff escaped his lips. He stepped uncomfortably close to Kat, eyes narrowed. "You and Roger are exactly the same."

Leia sobered at his sudden shift.

Kat blinked. "I'm not like Roger," she insisted, even though she'd never met the man.

Carlos gritted his jaw. "You go out of your way to start rumors about people."

"That's not fair," Leia said, stunned at how quickly the conversation had turned. "Kat's only trying to understand what happened." She turned to her friend, who appeared to have been struck mute. "Tell him, Kat."

"Tell 'em, Kat," Carlos mocked. "Tell 'em I'm right."

Kat stood rigid, her breathing shallow as she met Carlos's gaze head-on. "Why don't you tell me what you went to prison for?"

The corner of his mouth edged up. "Kidnapping the Easter Bunny." He dropped the smirk. "I've never met you before in my life. How is it your business?"

Kat retreated. "You're right. It's not." She smoothed her hair with a shaking hand.

But Carlos surged forward, once again closing the gap. His eyes flashed, cold as steel. "Get out of my camp."

"Let's go," Leia whispered.

"Go find someone else to gossip about," Carlos ordered, his voice echoing behind them as they beat a hasty retreat.

## CHAPTER
# THIRTEEN

Katherine's hands quivered as she and Leia made a brisk retreat across the snowy field, putting as much distance as they could between themselves and Carlos's camp. Her heart raced, and a chill that had nothing to do with the temperature seeped into her bones. She felt terribly wrong.

Exposed.

She plunged her hands into her pockets, her fingers pressing deep against the soft lining of her gloves.

"Hey, it's okay." Leia angled her head, trying to catch Katherine's eye.

Katherine fixed her gaze on the ice hotel ahead. She should be used to confrontation after years in the ER, handling difficult patients who cursed and threatened. The difference was, there, she knew she was right.

But in this situation, Carlos had a point. "I was a jerk. I should have kept my mouth shut."

"No." The firmness in Leia's voice made Katherine turn. "Paul's injured. Roger's probably dead. If someone's hurting people to win, we need to figure it out before anyone else gets hurt."

"That's what I thought until—" The knot in her stomach tightened.

"Look, we can avoid Carlos completely. Remember how I helped you avoid your ex in high school?"

Despite herself, Katherine's lips twitched. "I don't think a voodoo doll will work this time."

"Hey, he bolted every time I waved it around."

"I'm just encouraging you now," Katherine said dryly.

But Leia was on a roll. "I could do you one better this time. Maybe convince the hotel staff to dress up as yetis. They'll create a protective wall whenever Carlos shows up. He'll never know you're there."

A laugh escaped before Katherine could stop it. "Bonus points if you add a blanket fort for me to hide in with my yeti Secret Service detail."

"Complete with hot cocoa," Leia promised as they approached the arched wooden doors set within a wall of snow. "I mean, what are friends for if not to protect each other from grumpy ice sculptors?"

Warmth blossomed in Katherine's chest. "I'm lucky to have you. You know that?"

Leia squeezed her arm. "Just try to get rid of me."

"I keep trying," Katherine said, leaning toward her friend. "But then your bird calls, and you drag me to crazy places like this."

"Let that be a lesson." Leia pushed through the thick, insulating plastic strips.

They stepped into the enchanted forest lobby, where soft lights played beneath a tinkling frozen chandelier.

"Look." Leia pointed toward a back door. Beyond it, a bonfire crackled under the stars.

How had they missed that?

"Katherine, Leia! Over here."

Trishelle waved from an arched doorway while, behind her, John's grinning face peeked out from atop the slide. Snow clung to their pants. They'd clearly been at it a time or two.

"We heard you were looking for us," Trishelle called as John whooped on his way down.

Katherine hesitated. Carlos's words still stung. She'd never thought of herself as nosy or judgmental, but here she was, prying again.

Leia had no such reservations. "We ran into Caitlyn Wu at the spa. She wanted us to take a look at one of Roger's rooms from two years ago."

The year Amy didn't finish.

The year Roger's face met someone's fist.

"Oh, sure." Trishelle scrunched her nose. "Which theme was that?"

"No clue," Leia replied. "But Carlos seemed pretty upset about it. We were hoping you might know why."

Katherine felt a twinge of guilt. More gossip. Carlos was right. They just kept digging.

But it was too late to stop now.

"I have photos from every year on my phone," Trishelle offered.

"Two benches just opened up near the fireplace!" John interrupted, gesturing toward an ice-cave nook past the bar.

A terrifying-looking yeti guarded the entrance, its carved arm stretched across the arch. Natural icicles formed matted hair and spiky teeth.

Katherine ducked beneath the stalactites, even though they were well over her head. "Glad this guy isn't real. Ice sculptors are bad enough."

"He's the perfect head of security for your blanket fort." Leia slapped her on the back. "No one's getting past him."

"The cocoa is safe for sure." Katherine bumped Leia's shoulder.

Inside, fur-covered benches circled a gas fireplace. The flames cast dancing shadows on the icy walls. John and Trishelle claimed the spot by the door, while Katherine and Leia snagged the one next to them.

Katherine suppressed a shiver. Fur or no fur, she was sitting on a block of ice.

She shifted, recalling how her dad used to lovingly refer to her as 'bony butt.' At least Leia appeared content. Her layers had paid off at last.

Couples and groups filled all the other benches, their chatter filling the small space. Katherine's heart sank. With this crowd, they couldn't ask Trishelle about her photos or Roger's mysterious room.

"So?" Trishelle clasped her hands. "What do you think of your first competition?"

"It's intense," Katherine said, going for the bald truth.

"Fascinating," Leia said. "It seems like the teams are on edge, though. I mean, there was celebrating, but then…" Leia fidgeted with her ice cup. "Is it usually this tense in the camps?"

"Tense?" John's brow furrowed. "How so?"

Katherine lowered her voice. "At Larry's camp, they held this toast for Roger that felt more like a roast. They seemed ready to write him off as dead. Almost eager. It was a little strange. I'm not sure they liked Roger all that much."

"Well, nobody liked Roger." John's voice carried, drawing sideways glances. "And these are Manitobans. They know the odds of surviving this long in that weather."

Katherine cringed inwardly. So much for subtlety.

Trishelle shot him a fond smile. "Roger was..." She recrossed her legs. "Difficult. He ran his camp like a dictator and hated his team mixing with other competitors."

"He kicked one guy off for having lunch with another team," John added.

Katherine nodded. That tracked if Roger suspected sabotage.

"His team's making up for lost time now," Leia said. "The toast drew quite a crowd."

"Everyone wants to support Larry." Trishelle beamed.

John turned to his wife. "You know, this is the first year we've really got to know any of Roger's people."

"Larry's such a sweetheart," Trishelle gushed.

"He is," Leia agreed.

Wait. Katherine frowned. "Why would Roger keep his team from talking to you two? You're not even competitors."

"I have no idea," Trishelle said with a shrug. "Roger would chat with us plenty, but anytime we tried talking to his team, he'd shut it down. Maybe he didn't trust anyone."

John made a dismissive gesture with his drink. "Roger was always paranoid about anyone outside his team seeing his plans. Larry was telling me yesterday that Roger was even reluctant to show his own team unless there was an instruction they absolutely had to get right. He didn't trust any of them." His lips pressed into a thin line. "It must have been a difficult way to work. Very isolating, and for no reason."

There it was! That was the connection. Roger wasn't just suspicious of other teams around his equipment. He was territorial about his plans too. He had to have a reason to be so suspicious of everyone. Except for one thing that still didn't fit.

"If Roger was so paranoid about outsiders, why was he close with Alexi?" Katherine asked.

Talk about a double standard.

"They were best buds." Trishelle's voice held a note of irony. "At least until recently."

John snorted. "They'd go out drinking. Especially once the competition started. Alexi could barely function the next morning. Actually, this has been his best year yet. Amazing what you can do without a hangover."

"What about their falling-out?" Katherine pressed. "Alexi said something about Roger using his mother."

"Oh, that." Trishelle flicked a hand. "Roger would bet Alexi he couldn't finish an entire batch of his mama's homemade hooch. Alexi never backed down—family pride and all."

"Then one time, Roger made him call his mom afterward," John added. "Whatever they said in Russian, it broke Alexi. He stormed out, missed the first full day of competition."

Katherine whistled under her breath.

"Did he finish in time?" Leia asked.

"Barely scraped third. His sculpture almost lost its head, literally."

Katherine filed that away, then ventured, "Carlos seems to have his own issues with Roger. He said Roger was spreading rumors."

Trishelle's eyes widened. "He blames Roger for that? That gossip spread faster than free drinks on opening night."

"What gossip?" Leia leaned in.

Trishelle glanced around before whispering, "That Amy

was sleeping with Frank Fischer, the head judge, to win." She caught Katherine's shocked expression. "Completely baseless, of course."

"You never know," John mused.

"Please." Trishelle's braids swung as she shook her head. "First, it's Frank." Her nose crinkled as if that explained it. "Second, it's the same old story—one woman leads a team and suddenly she must be sleeping her way to the top. Never mind her devotion to Carlos."

"I see what you mean," Leia said, making a face.

"Hold on." Katherine held up a hand. "Who's Frank?"

Trishelle pointed to a wiry man with fiery red hair hunched over a notebook, his thick glasses fogging with each breath. He scribbled with a pencil that looked tiny in his gloved hand. He paused only to push his glasses up his nose before they slid right back down.

Sweat dotted his forehead despite the cold.

He seemed entirely absorbed in his work, oblivious to the party.

Katherine noticed they were now alone in the ice cave. Everyone else had migrated to the bar. Everyone except Frank.

"Bob!" John raised his hand to catch the attention of a tall man in furry boots walking past. "Excuse me," he added, standing to greet his friend.

Leia nudged Katherine. "I nominate that guy to join the yeti security team. He's got the fur down pat."

"He can design their uniforms," Katherine quipped.

"We should go mingle," Trishelle said, eyeing the crowd.

"I'm cozy here on the ice bench," Katherine said, stretching the truth a little. *Okay, a lot.* She ignored her frozen butt and plowed forward. "About that room Roger designed two years ago. You said you had photos?"

"Right." Trishelle's attention drifted to Bob's companion, who wore an equally obnoxious pink fur coat that gave yeti man a run for his money. "I haven't seen the Albertsons in ages. Here—" She unlocked her phone and handed it to Katherine. "My password is 1-2-3-4 if it locks on you."

"Seriously?" Leia asked, poised for a security talk.

*Go with it*, Katherine thought, silently willing her friend to play along.

"I'll need it back in a minute," Trishelle said, already headed to greet her friends. "We'll want to take a reunion photo."

"A minute is all we need," Katherine promised, hoping she was right.

## CHAPTER
# FOURTEEN

Kat and Leia huddled close, their heads nearly touching as Leia's fingers flew across the screen, scrolling back one year. Two. "Trishelle has more pictures than the Louvre."

"Use the search feature," Kat urged.

"Almost there." Leia kept scrolling past landscapes and countless shots of a tuxedo cat.

*Can't fault her for that one.*

Then she hit the hotel's opening night two years ago.

Her heart sank. Every room. Every hall. Every inch of the hotel was documented in excruciating detail.

"How are we supposed to know which one is Roger's?" Kat asked over her shoulder.

"Forget that. How do we look through all of these before she wants her phone back?" Leia stole a quick glance at Trishelle, who had luckily collected another couple to talk with.

Sure, she had new friends to keep her busy, but how long until she'd want to capture the moment?

Kat jolted. "There." She pointed. "That's Roger."

Leia zoomed in on a man crouched in an icy corner. Broad cheeks, scruffy blond hair. The same face from the coffee table book. "Got him."

They leaned closer, studying the room. "On the wall," Kat said. "A bird...cuddling a carp?"

Below it, carved text read *A bird can fall in love with a fish, but where would they live?*

"Oooh. Are we talking forbidden love?" Leia suggested.

The next photo showed a nest sculpted into the wall above the bed. A lovebird nestled against a fish with triangular scales, its head glowing red under LED lights. Maybe it was supposed to be a salmon.

"More birds and fish," Kat murmured.

Then Leia saw it. "That's Amy." Leia lifted the phone higher for a closer look. The lovebird's feathers fanned out around its head and slashed across its forehead, matching Amy's distinct hairstyle.

Kat inhaled sharply. "I can't unsee it now. Amy in bed with a fish. Fischer. Redheaded Frank Fischer. Wow, that's not exactly subtle."

Leia zoomed in on a lotus flower blooming beside the bird. "I wonder what that signifies."

"We'll research it later," Kat promised. "In the meantime, scroll back. I want to see what Roger was carving near the bottom of that first wall."

Leia returned to the first photo. Roger's face was a mess—swollen eye, split lip. Someone had done a number on him. Crouched in the corner, he carved a broken spiderweb into the snow.

"A broken web." Leia's stomach turned. "He didn't just target Amy. That web—it's Carlos's tattoo. Roger went for both of them."

"Oh, that's low." Kat grimaced. "And incredibly crass."

"High effort, too. To make it the theme of a room." Talk about a dedication to pettiness.

"More than that." Kat straightened. "The rooms were first revealed at opening night. Was Roger actually finishing his room during the party?"

"Maybe Trishelle got early access." She'd had it tonight for the competition.

"No, look. The previous photos are from the opening party. He worked on this in front of guests." Kat tapped the screen. "He arrived late just to needle Amy."

"That's it!" Leia said. The rumor had spread that night. "But why did it affect Amy so badly?" She flipped through the photos, then stopped, her finger hovering above the screen. "Kat, look at Amy's piece from that year."

Kat leaned in, squinting. "What on earth?"

The sculpture was nothing like Amy's style. It looked as if they'd carved something from an existing statue.

"Looks like she scrapped her original idea and created a water fountain out of the mess, like Larry and the broken mirror." Leia traced the shape. "Could've started as a lotus flower. Same base, same nodes. But the water..." She turned the phone sideways. "It's all wrong. Chunky, not flowing. Like she rushed to carve something new and botched it."

Kat tilted her head. "Squint and the water looks like lovebirds. I'll bet that was her plan. Two lovebirds above a lotus."

"Redesigning mid-competition?" Leia winced. "With those rumors flying, I doubt anyone offered to help."

"No wonder Carlos helped Larry instead," Kat said. "Old wounds, but he's the bigger person."

"So Roger arrives late, taunts Amy with his room art, and when the rumors start, she panics and changes her sculpture to avoid looking like she's sleeping with the head judge."

"Jerry Springer, step aside."

Leia's blood boiled. Roger wasn't just a jerk; he was a radioactive dumpster fire of a human being. "No wonder Carlos was fuming. Could Carlos have wanted revenge? Maybe he sabotaged Roger's team."

Before Kat could answer, Trishelle appeared with her husband. "Phone, please? We're heading out."

"Already?" Leia handed it over, wishing for even five minutes more. "The party's just getting started," she added as a cheer erupted from the raucous crowd at the bar.

John pulled Trishelle close. "We've got a hot tub date with destiny."

"In our private tub." Trishelle giggled, leaning into him.

"Lucky you," Leia said, catching the not-so-subtle hint.

"While we're not extending a tub invite," John said, giving his wife a jovial squeeze, "you two should try the tub by our cabins. You'll warm up your sleeping bag faster if your body temperature is raised. It'll make for a more comfortable night in your frozen room."

"Thanks for the tip," Leia said as John's wife dragged him away.

"Less talking, more canoodling," Trishelle said as her voice trailed off.

Leia sighed. "Relationship goals, right there."

"I want to follow them," Kat grumbled. At Leia's look, she added, "Not to the love tub. But there go our photos and our last shot at clues."

"And come morning, it's all over," Leia said.

But they couldn't quit. They'd already uncovered too much—the wrecked car, Amy's past, the inner workings of the competition.

## CHAPTER FOURTEEN

Leia burrowed deeper into her coat.

They were close to something big. She could feel it.

Kat rubbed her temples. "Maybe we should call it a night."

But Leia wasn't listening. Her gaze fixed on Frank Fischer sitting alone at the end of the bar, lost in his drink. "What if Amy truly loved him?"

"What?" Kat's head snapped up.

Stranger things had happened.

The pieces clicked into place. Roger's beaten face, the broken web, Amy's hastily altered sculpture. "The timing fits," she said, already moving.

Kat scrambled after her. "Fits what?"

"Frank could be Amy's mysterious 'Red.'"

Kat's eyes lit up. "Oh, I like this."

"What if he's the missing piece?"

"You had me at Red."

They navigated through the crowd. Frank's fiery red hair stood out like a beacon, a stark contrast to the thick, fogged-up glasses obscuring his eyes.

"We could be wrong," Kat whispered, watching him chew his pencil.

"Don't rule him out. Amy was heartbroken before Carlos, but they started dating two years ago." Leia lowered her voice. "It could be an older affair Roger exposed."

Frank sipped his drink, only to choke on it, sputtering and coughing.

"I've done that," Leia said, catching Kat's look. "He must be magnetic in person. Some girls dig nerdy guys. I'm exhibit A."

Or maybe Amy had truly bizarre taste in men.

"Alrighty, then," Kat said. "Let's charm some secrets out of this wizard."

"Operation Red is a go."

"Do we get code names?"

"You wish."

Despite the crowd, Frank sat in his own bubble of empty ice benches.

"Hi there," Leia chirped, popping Frank's bubble. "I'm Leia, and this is Kat. We've been dying to meet you."

Frank wiped his nose. "Okay." He looked a little scared.

Off to a stellar start.

Kat tried, "How long have you been judging these festivals? Bet you've seen it all."

Frank pushed up his glasses. "Yeah." He yawned.

"Any favorite sculptures?" Leia asked.

Frank stared blankly, his glasses sliding down once more. "My favorites are the winners. I'm a judge, remember?"

"Riiight." Leia smiled, her cheer sounding fake even to herself.

She caught Kat's *I told you so* look.

Leia planted an elbow on the bar. "Any good festival gossip? We love a good story."

Frank blinked. "I went ice fishing yesterday. And this morning," he added, showing signs of life. "The ice finally hit a foot thick."

"Is that significant?" Kat ventured after an awkward pause.

Frank looked at her like she'd grown a second head. "The ice on the lake needs to be four inches to walk on, and one foot to support an ice shanty."

"I see." Leia blinked. Time for the nuclear option, a dad joke. "I mean...*icy* what you did there."

Frank's confusion deepened.

"Ice fishing...icy... Never mind. You seem passionate about the sport," she added, looking for a silver lining.

A ghost of a smile haunted Frank's lips. "Only me, alone for hours. Waiting for a bite. It's thrilling."

"Ever take anyone special out there?" Kat probed.

Frank grimaced. "That would defeat the purpose."

"I just remembered Trishelle and John need us in their hot tub," Leia blurted.

"Yes, they're probably lonely," Kat added, backpedaling for all she was worth.

"Great meeting you," Leia called over her shoulder.

Frank waved, looking as relieved as she felt.

"When you're right, you're right," Leia said when they made it outside.

"I didn't want to be *that* right," Kat said. "Well, that was a dead end. Now what?"

"Hot tub?"

"Hot tub."

A short time later, Leia shivered and pulled her robe more tightly around her. A light breeze swirled, and the sky was alive with a thousand stars.

Kat bolted ahead, her feet pounding the steps. "Last one in sings 'I'm a Barbie Girl'!"

"That's how you cracked your skull at Splashland!" Leia called as Kat skidded on the snow and nearly lost a flip-flop.

"Worth it," Kat said as Leia hoofed it down the snowy path toward the hot tub nestled between their cabin and the others. "That's the summer Billy Parker noticed me."

"Because you were bleeding on him."

Kat tossed her robe and sank into the water. "Fortune favors the bold."

"Or the concussed." Leia joined her.

Warmth enveloped them as colored lights danced beneath the bubbles.

Leia let out a small sigh as she sank in up to her neck. "I guess it all worked out in the end."

"Like this tub is working out." Kat settled back. "I could stay forever."

*Not a bad idea.* Leia settled into a corner and watched steam rise into the night, letting the jets work their magic.

Kat's eyes fluttered shut. "I don't care what Frank Fischer says; this beats ice fishing any day."

Steam mixed with cold air, creating tiny snowflakes that kissed their cheeks.

"I'm glad we met Frank," Kat said, "but there's no way he inspired Amy's heartbreak."

"Maybe she's a secret ice fishing champion." Leia snorted, the bubbles tickling her nose.

Kat sobered. "Roger was cruel spreading that rumor. It hurt Amy, Carlos, even Frank."

"No arguments here," Leia said, recalling Roger's bruised face.

Kat suddenly splashed upright. "What if we've got this backward?"

"I'm listening."

"We assumed someone wanted to sabotage Roger." Kat pulled herself onto the bench next to Leia. "But Roger's been hurting all the other teams. What if he's the only saboteur?"

"So he's been getting Alexi drunk—"

"To weaken his game. Alexi caught on after the call to his mother. That's why he cut contact."

Leia slapped the water, sending a spray of droplets skyward. "Then Roger started the Amy rumor."

Kat nodded vigorously. "His eye was injured. He

couldn't read his plans clearly, and he was afraid he wouldn't perform well." She pushed wet bangs from her face. "So he changed the theme of his room to spread rumors about Amy, forcing her to alter her sculpture mid-competition. That's why she didn't finish."

"He basically eliminated her as competition." Leia swished her arms through the water. "No wonder Roger didn't want his team talking to anyone else. They're all decent guys. Larry, Paul—they'd never cheat. Look how hard they worked, knowing they'd lose."

"Just for the love of it."

"And helping others when they could."

"If they knew Roger was undermining teams, they'd have quit."

Leia sank lower. "Larry might've known. He said Roger had done things he shouldn't be proud of." She frowned. "But if Roger was the saboteur, why was he so paranoid about being sabotaged?"

"Maybe the other teams wanted revenge."

"But why target Amy's straps too?"

"Let's look at the timeline," Kat suggested. "In Roger's camp, the straps were loosened on Monday and Tuesday. He had Paul check them. Then on Thursday, the buckle broke."

"Wait, wait, wait, wait!" Leia splashed. "The broken buckle was on the orange strap. All the other straps in Roger's camp were green!"

"And?"

"When we arrived and the arm was going up on Alexi's goddess, those straps were orange. Larry said they borrowed equipment. The only equipment I didn't see up for grabs in the workshop was extra straps. Larry borrowed the faulty orange strap from Alexi."

Kat sat straight up. "Alexi's and Amy's straps were actually sabotaged, but in Roger's camp they were just loosened—which he caught each morning. He pointed it out to his team and made a show of fixing them. That's truly devious."

"He kept his team suspicious, deflected attention, and hurt the other teams without risking his own work." Leia felt that familiar rush of certainty, that ping of excitement when she knew she had something right.

"Okay. Then why not mess with Eric's straps?"

"Maybe he did and we don't know about it," Leia said. "I think Roger's been sabotaging competitions for years."

Kat's expression darkened. "If someone had been screwing you over that long..."

Leia drummed her fingers against the bench. "I wouldn't want to *kill* him."

"Neither would I. But maybe things got out of hand. Or..." Kat paused.

"Spill it."

"Some people *are* killers," Kat said. "The longer he's missing, the bleaker it looks."

Leia couldn't argue. This was a real motive. "The timing fits. Alexi called his mom the same year Roger got the black eye. If Alexi beat him up, that's felony assault. Bye-bye American visa."

"He'd have to return home suddenly." Kat popped a bubble. "And if it was Carlos—"

"He'd go back to prison." Yikes. "Would he risk that over Roger taunting Amy?"

Kat shot her a look. "Carlos does have a temper."

"So does Alexi."

They fell quiet.

Leia ran wet hands through her hair. "Let's think this

through. We know Roger carved that message about Amy in a room."

"And we're sleeping in one of his rooms tonight." Kat's voice dropped lower.

Leia inched closer. "What if this year, he couldn't resist leaving another message? Something to taunt whoever attacked him."

"Like blackmail carved in ice." Kat's voice cracked. "If he knew who hurt him—"

"He'd want leverage. Insurance." It all made sense. "A hidden message that would push his attacker to make a fatal mistake."

"Only it could have pushed someone to kill."

Leia stared at Kat. "Do you know what this means? If we're right, the writing will be on the wall."

Kat's jaw dropped. "Holy moly." Her eyes lit up. "We need to get to bed."

*Heck yes.*

Kat's face fell. "One problem."

"Name it."

Kat eyed their robes. "We're wet. Those robes are freezing."

"Good thing we're badasses." Leia splashed her. "Come on."

## CHAPTER
# FIFTEEN

Fiery torches lit the way as Katherine and Leia booked it down the snowy path toward the ice hotel.

"I can't believe we made it out of the hot tub and into our jammies in two minutes," Leia said, catching her breath.

It had been more like ten, but who was counting? "We are rockstars!" Katherine shouted into the night, her voice echoing across the frozen landscape.

"Wait, wait, wait." Leia fell behind, wrestling with her jam-packed overnight bag. "I need to check—"

Katherine walked backward to face her. "You've got everything. Trust me."

Leia had packed like they were catching the last flight out of Casablanca.

Katherine had changed into her pajamas, dried her hair, put on warm socks, donned a stocking cap and her ski jacket, and left the rest in her room. She was more than ready. In fact, she'd managed with less before.

But Leia was on a roll. "Extra warm jammies in case

these aren't enough. Check. Long underwear. Check. Arctic-rated socks—" Her friend searched furiously.

"Check." Katherine tucked her hands into the pockets of her parka. "I saw you pack them."

"Good." Leia readjusted the bag over her shoulder, her hand instinctively reaching up to make sure her stocking cap was secure. "These days, I'd forget my head if it weren't attached." She quickened her pace to catch up. "Oh, and keep your cell phone close to your body tonight, or it'll die on you."

"Already on it." Katherine patted her pocket. The battery needed to stay warm.

Leia had reminded her already.

"We should put them in airplane mode too. They'll drain searching for a signal under a snow roof. If one of our phones goes out, that's bad. If both die...disaster." Leia took the lead as the ice hotel came into view. "We'll need to take pictures if Roger did leave a clue behind in our room." The crowds had thinned to just a few people in the courtyard.

"Let's not get our hopes up," Kat cautioned.

"Too late." Leia gave her a playful nudge.

They greeted Ian as they passed. The wiry foreman stood next to one of the flatbed work trucks she'd seen them use to haul ice. This time, he'd loaded it up with rolled sleeping bags. Katherine watched him toss a bright blue one onto the pile.

"Are those for us?" she asked, slowing her pace. She hadn't thought they'd need to carry their own bags in.

"We really should have watched the video," Leia said.

Ian grinned, his cheeks ruddy with the cold. "You girls are doing great." He tossed another sleeping bag into the truck. "I'm just getting a head start on cleanup. These are from folks who've already left the ice hotel for the night."

## CHAPTER FIFTEEN

"We're later than I thought," Katherine said.

"Most arrive as soon as the hotel opens for guests. Some stay." He cast a wistful look at the pile. "Many reserve rooms in the ice hotel but change their minds rather quickly."

Truly? "Why wouldn't everyone stay?" It was expensive. And a one-of-a-kind experience.

Ian gave a regretful shrug. "Some say it's too cold. Others get claustrophobic surrounded by snowy walls. Some enjoy the novelty for the evening but prefer their cabins or a room in the resort to sleep." He gestured helplessly. "Breaks my heart. But I am glad they came, even briefly."

"I'm sure they loved it while they were there," Katherine assured him. He and his team had put so much effort into creating the hotel. It honestly was a labor of love. It seemed like all he wanted was for others to experience it.

"Your hall in particular has had lots of departures tonight. You're the only ones left." He tossed another bag. "At least you won't have to worry about noisy neighbors," he added with a rueful grin.

"We can't wait," Leia said as they headed out.

Katherine slowed as they approached the glowing ice hotel. It was even prettier late at night under a vast canopy of stars. "What would Jen say about this?"

Leia shot her a fond look. "She'd have loved it."

"I love it, too."

They stepped through the plastic flaps guarding the entrance into the near-deserted lobby.

"Amazing how fast it cleared out," Leia observed.

"We spent more time in the hot tub than we realized." Katherine's fingers still felt a bit pruney.

"Not hard to do."

Katherine checked her watch. Only guests who'd paid to stay in the ice hotel were allowed at this hour.

The hotel lay still as a solitary bartender closed up shop.

They made their way to the rooms. "We're so late," Katherine said, her voice absorbed by the snowy hallway.

Ian was right. Katherine and Leia didn't hear a sound as they navigated the corridor.

While Leia had made her second bathroom trip—just to be sure—Katherine had reviewed their opening night photos. She hadn't spotted anything damning in Roger's other room. Except for the crime against cheese.

They reached the spot where Leia had fallen.

Leia halted to examine the sphinx's nose. Meanwhile, Katherine crouched down, pressing a gloved hand against the once-soft spot on the floor. "Looks like they fixed it." Interesting, considering she and Leia had forgotten to report it.

"And nobody fixed the sphinx's nose," Leia said. "That means I didn't break it. What a relief."

"For you and your bank account." Katherine stood, noting the patched finger marks on the sphinx's shoulder. "I wonder why the floor was soft in the first place."

"I just want to see our room," Leia said, eyeing the cerulean curtain.

The sign outside read:

*The Tomb*

*By Roger Cullins*

She exchanged a look with Leia. "Well, that's not ominous at all."

"It's better than cheese."

This was it.

Katherine swept aside the curtain. Ancient drums and haunting flutes filled the air. A giant Egyptian sarcophagus loomed over their bed, carved from solid ice and illuminated from within.

"Holy moly," Leia breathed.

"I feel like we just stumbled into King Tut's tomb."

A glass-encased fireplace cast flickering shadows onto the carved walls. Their boots crunched as they approached the bed, which rested on an altar adorned with ice scarabs. Across the room, an ice table and bench mimicked crates overflowing with pharaoh's treasures. A towering Anubis emerged from one corner, its jackal head tilted toward them, striding across a wall covered in hieroglyphics.

"Look at this." Leia marveled at two palm trees arching over an oasis, their fronds reaching toward the ceiling. Three yellow lights brightened the desert scene, while a life-sized camel sauntered toward the door, its icy hump glistening in the firelight. "Roger had a field day."

No doubt about it.

But did he leave any messages behind?

They captured everything on their phones, taking photos and video from every angle.

"I wish I could send these to Nick," Leia said, searching for a signal.

"I don't have any bars on my phone, either," Katherine said while Leia snapped a photo of her checking.

And while Leia documented the Anubis, Katherine struck a pose next to the hieroglyphics.

"I think I was an Egyptian queen in a past life," she said, running a gloved hand behind her stocking cap.

Leia laughed. "Well, you do like cats."

Still, something about the room nagged at Katherine. Roger had gone to elaborate lengths here. "What does it mean?"

Leia retrieved her bag from the doorway. "I honestly don't see anything strange."

That was the problem. "Let's go over it one more time."

Leia dropped the bag by the bed, and they set about inspecting every inch of the room, scrutinizing the carvings and hieroglyphics. Searching every scratch in the icy footboard, every etch on the palm trees. Katherine even peeked inside the treasure crates.

"If there's a secret message here, Roger deserves an Oscar for hiding it," Leia said from behind the Anubis.

Katherine examined the area under the bed, finding only a nest of wires and a couple of speakers. "I'm not seeing anything that points a finger at Alexi *or* Carlos."

"It's a tomb," Leia said, searching the corners. "He could easily have added spiderwebs." Exactly like he'd done in the corner in the room where Roger had been blackmailing Amy.

But here, where they belonged?

Nothing.

Katherine sat on the snowy floor, tucking her ski jacket under her flannel pajamas. The photos from Trishelle's phone kept coming back to her, that blatant message about Amy, unmistakable to anyone who knew her. And the red fish could only mean Mr. Fischer.

None of it made sense.

"I don't see anything pointing to Carlos in here."

Katherine hugged her knees. She'd been sure they'd find something in their room tonight. Maybe she'd read one too many mysteries.

"Need a hand?" Leia offered.

They stood together, taking in the elaborate chamber.

"Maybe the Amy thing was a one-off," Leia said,

studying the ceiling. "The cheese room wasn't exactly cryptic either."

"You're probably right." Katherine hesitated. "He could have gotten drunk and wrecked his own car."

But that didn't sit right. Something had felt wrong from the moment she'd looked into that open passenger door. She just couldn't pin down what.

"Hey," Leia said, "even if this is a wild-goose chase, and all we learn is that ice can kill you several different ways, I'm still having a lot of fun with you."

"Me too." She couldn't help but smile. "I wish Jen were here. She would have loved running around an ice hotel."

"And spa."

"Falling while snowshoeing."

"Getting stuck on the slide."

"And now this." Katherine gestured at their frozen surroundings. She never imagined having a sleepover in an ice tomb.

Leia rubbed her hands together. "Let's get in those sleeping bags before we end up as stiff as those ladies on the walls."

A pair of arctic sleeping bags lay rolled up on the bed. Katherine quickly laid hers flat and unzipped the side. The sleeping bag was snug, but not uncomfortable. Likely designed to retain heat. She zipped hers up as Leia stuffed a pair of long underwear into hers, along with an extra pair of socks and a sweatshirt. "In case I get cold," she said, shivering in her pj's.

"Just get in." Katherine was surprised at how cozy it was in her little cocoon. "You'll feel better."

"I can't sleep with lights and music," Leia said, scanning the room. "Did you see an Off switch anywhere?"

She hadn't. And she was reluctant to leave her warm

nest to help Leia find it. "There are wires under the bed. Maybe it's on the frame."

Leia found the controls in the gap between the platform and the ice. She killed the music and the main lights, leaving them swimming in the gentle flickering light of the fire and the glow from the lights embedded in the walls.

She dove onto the mattress and shimmied into her bag, zipping it to her chin. "This is wild," she said, tucking her pillow inside. The back of her bag covered her head like a hood.

"If we pull these drawstrings tight enough, I'll bet only our noses will stick out." Katherine reached for the strings to try.

"Not yet." Leia shifted to face her. "I'm too keyed up to sleep."

"Me too." Katherine snuggled deeper. It felt like their old sleepovers—just them with nowhere else to be. No responsibilities. Nothing to do but hang out and enjoy each other's company.

The entire trip had been that way.

"Why is having fun so hard now?" Katherine asked.

Leia propped her head on her chin. "What do you mean?"

It was hard to explain. "I don't feel like the same person I was as a kid. I've gotten more controlled," she said, trying to put a name on it. "More focused. I do grownup things. I go by Katherine."

"We can always change that back."

Katherine laughed. "Truth be told, I'm afraid I'm not fun anymore."

Leia smiled. "I hate to burst your bubble, but you've always been a detail-oriented, persnickety control freak. It's one of the things I love about you."

"No," Katherine protested, but part of her wanted to cheer. "I used to laugh more. But I can't be that way and still do my job and keep my life together. Adult life is hard." She'd been saying that to herself for years. "Traveling the world volunteering is hard, but what I do is important." And as she said it, she realized she'd laughed more in the last few days than she had in the past year, and it felt *good*.

She wasn't sure what to do with that.

"Well, I have fun with you," Leia said simply.

"Me too."

"I'm sorry I've been so focused on all this ice-sculpting drama."

"What do you mean?" Katherine propped herself up on an elbow.

"Maybe we're crazy and chasing shadows. I don't know." Leia flopped on her back in her bag. "I see so many crime stories where I have to do the fact-checking, and I always think, if there was just one more piece of the puzzle, one more little detail someone noticed, that maybe the truth would come out and the crime could be solved. Then the victim would get justice, you know?"

"You're a good person." Katherine snuggled down, facing her.

They fell into a comfortable silence. Leia studied the room, and Katherine thought about how lucky she was to have been dragged into this crazy adventure. How she wouldn't have done it for herself. And how she didn't have to.

She had her friend.

Her eyelids grew heavy.

"Kat—" Leia gasped. "I could be wrong, but I don't think I am."

"What?"

Leia's eyes darted from the ceiling to the walls. "The timing doesn't line up."

She was going to need to give her more than that. "What do you mean?"

"Well..." Leia flipped to face Katherine again. "If we're assuming Roger put clues in this room to manipulate Carlos because Carlos beat him up for starting rumors..."

"Yes?"

"And that assault conviction could send him back to jail." Leia unzipped her bag and sat up. "The timing doesn't line up. Roger had that black eye while he was still carving the lovebird room—before he started the rumor."

"You're right." Katherine bolted upright. Leia flicked the main lights back on. "Carlos has a temper, and he holds a grudge." She struggled to get her zipper down before she strangled herself. "But Carlos would have had zero problem with Roger before that room."

"Exactly." Leia yanked Katherine's zipper down and freed her. "Roger didn't interact with the other teams at all, and it was Carlos's first year. They barely knew each other."

"Right." It was clear as day. "Also Carlos is sober."

"How do you know?"

"He was drinking O'Doul's at the celebration. Have you tasted that stuff? Nobody drinks that unless they don't drink at all."

"I can't believe you noticed that too. Wait, no. I can." Leia reached back for her sleeping bag and wrapped it around her shoulders. "So Roger would've been suspicious if Carlos showed up wanting to share a bottle of tequila with him."

"Exactly." Now, what did it all mean?

Leia thought for a long, hard minute. "If Carlos didn't

beat Roger up, do you think Alexi is supposed to be the camel?"

"I'm not following."

"Camels drink a lot."

Maybe, but that was a stretch.

Katherine slipped into her boots to check the carving. "Roger would've made the camel drink from the oasis if that were the case. But it's walking away."

"True. And John said Alexi was drunk Tuesday night. Would he have been sober enough to trick Roger?" She frowned, scanning the room. "And if he did offer Roger something spiked, why tequila instead of his mother's special drink?"

They fell silent, lost in thought.

"Then I'm stumped." Katherine returned to her bag. "Who else would have had a problem with Roger? Maybe he did decide to drink half a bottle of tequila and drive off a cliff."

They settled down back to back, Leia facing the hieroglyphs, Katherine staring at the looming sarcophagus.

"Roger was obsessed with the feather of Ma'at," Leia said. "There must be ten of them over here."

Katherine rolled over to see. "How many times did you check out that Egypt book in third grade?"

"Too many. Plus that Nefertiti research for the Burke Museum article sent me down some rabbit holes."

"Which one is the feather of Ma'at?"

"That curly thing. It's the symbol of the goddess of truth and justice."

Katherine studied the etching of a winged woman with a feather in her hair, kneeling beside an unbalanced scale. Anubis, the god of death, knelt on the other side. "Who's the girl with wings? An angel?"

"That's Ma'at herself, the goddess of justice." Leia nearly fell off the bed. "Look at the scales. Wheat on the low side, and a stone on the high side. They're unbalanced."

They stared at each other.

*The scales had been tipped.*

Leia unzipped. Katherine sat up. They turned to the sarcophagus. For the first time, they noticed it wasn't a pharaoh, but a queen—with a single thick braid falling down her left shoulder.

"It's..." Katherine looked to Leia, who appeared as stunned as she felt. "That's Rebecca."

## CHAPTER
# SIXTEEN

Leia wrestled with her sleeping bag, kicking it off. The cold air barely registered. "Roger is saying Rebecca's death wasn't an accident." It was written plain as day on the wall. "He's saying the scales were tipped."

"As in someone deliberately collapsed the sculpture that killed Rebecca." Kat sat back. "If Roger's telling the truth, if Rebecca was murdered—"

"Who caused it to fall?"

"And why?" Kat ran a hand through her hair. "We need to figure out who had a motive."

"Wait." Leia tossed a pillow out of her lap. "If Roger was manipulating people to win, why expose a murder? Why does he care? Unless—"she stared at Kat—"unless he did it himself."

"No." Kat slipped into her boots, leaving them unlaced. "I mean, he put it on the wall." She began to pace. "A killer isn't going to draw attention to the crime." She blew on her hands as if she'd just realized she was standing in an ice cave in her pajamas. "This reminds me of *Hamlet*."

Leia shot her a quizzical look. *Antony and Cleopatra* seemed more fitting given the setting.

"Junior year—the play within a play. The king had poisoned his brother. Hamlet staged a performance to reveal the king's guilt without anyone else understanding." Kat retreated to the bed, facing Leia. "Hamlet knew if he could provoke him, the king would reveal his own guilt." She shivered and retreated into her sleeping bag. "That's what this room is. Roger knew something about Rebecca's accident. And he was trying to provoke the killer."

"The play within a play." A realization struck Leia. "It goes deeper."

"How?"

"The play within a play was called *The Mousetrap*."

Kat's jaw dropped. "The giant wedge of cheese. It's been a clue all along."

"The cheese isn't just a shape." Leia dove for her bag, rummaging through it like a crazy person, and maybe she was. "It's about balance." She emerged with a crumpled notepad rife with scribbled equations. "I need to show you something."

"Is that—"

"My notes from the accident video."

"I can't believe you packed everything."

"Bet you're glad now."

Leia laid the notepad on the bed between them, her fingers tracing the cascading equations. "I thought we might need to take notes." With shaky hands, she sketched a wedge under her diagram. "That's how it happened."

"The team would have noticed a chunk of ice shoved under their sculpture."

"True."

"And there was no wedge under the carving. The base was flat. We saw it on the news clip."

"Was it?" Leia pulled out the memorial book from her bag.

"Seriously?" Kat was both horrified and impressed. "Did you pack the coffee pot too?"

"No, even though we could use it." Leia flipped to Rebecca's picture. "Look at the sport drink on the base of the scale they're carving."

"Oh, wow." Kat skimmed a finger over the photo. "It's not level. And Rebecca's boot—look how far it's sinking into the snow."

"Exactly." Leia snapped the book shut. "It's just like when I tripped in the hole that had been filled with loose snow. The killer didn't shove a wedge under the sculpture. He cut one out!"

Kat leaned back, processing. "So half the statue was balanced on solid-packed ground." She positioned the notebook half on, half off the icy headboard. "And the other half—"

"Was on a soft spot in the snow. Disguised to look solid."

"Make a large enough cut in the sculpture on the solid side, and the change in weight—" Kat gently lifted the notebook.

It flipped, landing between them on the bed.

Kat ran a hand over her face. "The keys to the snow-moving equipment are hanging in the workshop. Anyone could access them." She dropped her hand. "But someone would notice a Bobcat digging around another team's site."

"Unless they were digging really late at night."

"About the same time Roger returned from the bar," Kat finished.

Their eyes met.

Leia's heart raced, sweat beading on her forehead despite the chill. She didn't want to believe Rebecca was murdered, but the evidence was undeniable.

A knot formed in her stomach as the pieces fell into place.

"Think about it," she continued, her throat tight. "Roger stumbles back from the bar and sees someone on a Bobcat in the Hardneys' area. He recognizes them, but he stays quiet. Maybe he's too drunk to realize something's wrong."

"Then days later, the accident happens." Kat's voice dropped. "And Roger remembers what he saw."

"So he blackmails the killer." Leia's pulse quickened. "The triangles, the wedges—they're his way of saying 'I know what you did.'" She took a shaky breath. "But this year, something changed. Tuesday night, Roger leaves the party suddenly. He had to meet someone."

"The killer offers Roger a drink—"

"Which Roger never refuses." Leia's hands clenched. "Once he's incapacitated, the killer drives him to the edge of the lake and makes sure he veers off the road." She swallowed hard. "It's a death sentence."

"A perfect accident." Kat frowned. "But the sculpture collapse... I don't get it. A massive hole would make stacking impossible. How do you time something like that?"

"You'd need precise blueprints for perfect balance—"

Kat stared at her. "You'd need to be a former engineer."

"And you'd need to know exactly where the hole is," Leia whispered, "because you dug it out yourself."

"In your own camp."

The ice hotel suddenly felt a whole lot colder.

## CHAPTER
# SEVENTEEN

"Why though?" Katherine's mind raced, the cold reality of their discovery settling in. "Why would he do it?"

He seemed too nice. Too much a part of this place. He could go anywhere he wanted, take anything he wanted. No one would even suspect.

He could even be inside the hotel with them at this very moment.

Katherine's lungs constricted as she fumbled for her phone. She'd tucked it into her long underwear to preserve the battery.

Five percent left.

She could have sworn she'd had more.

"It can't be Eric," Leia was saying as if voicing it would make it true. "He's too sweet, and he was devastated by Rebecca's death."

She hated to say it, but, "Feelings aren't facts."

"Maybe, but he hasn't won since then. You saw him. He was too broken. He needed Rebecca. Roger didn't need to take him out of the competition."

"Let me see that book." Leia slid it over to her. "Also, can you check and see if you have a phone connection?"

She hoped they could catch a signal this time. She refused to dwell on what could happen if they had no way to call for help.

While Leia searched her sleeping bag, Katherine flipped to the Hardney team photo. Eric stood out in his bright red toque, grinning while his teammates looked miserable. "Look at the date. This picture was taken at the first competition without Rebecca. Eric doesn't look too broken up, considering his wife died in that exact same spot the year before."

Leia scootched over to look, her mouth forming a grim line. "Okay, but to your point, that's not proof. Everyone grieves differently."

She had a point. She turned the book over, tracing Amy's name embossed in gold on the back.

"Ten percent power," Leia reported, holding up her phone. "The cold's draining the battery faster than I expected."

Katherine tucked her phone into her bra, hoping it was warmer there. She shivered against the cold metal and glass, eyeing the decorative curtain barring their door. There wasn't any deadbolt on a curtain. "Trishelle said Amy made these books to honor Rebecca. But Caitlyn told us they weren't friends. That they'd only met once, at Rebecca's last competition."

The one where she'd died.

Leia leafed through the book. "They shared a passion."

"Perhaps too much." Katherine lowered her voice. "Maybe she felt guilty."

Leia looked up. "What do you mean?"

"Amy's bad breakup happened right after Rebecca died. What if they're connected?"

Leia paused on Eric's team photo.

"What if Eric was 'Red'?" Katherine traced the red toque he wore in the photo. The word *Flambé* was embroidered in bold script across the front.

Leia's eyes widened. "Eric the Red. Caitlyn said Red was a cheater. I thought she meant Red cheated on Amy, but what if he cheated on Rebecca *with* Amy?"

"Remember what Caitlyn said about Amy's depression after the breakup?"

"If Amy thought their affair caused Rebecca's death—" Leia shivered. "No wonder she wouldn't want to talk about it."

"And it could be more complex," Katherine added. "Rebecca may have known, or at least suspected. No wonder they didn't get along."

"If Rebecca knew," Leia said slowly, "that could be why she was killed."

"How do you mean?"

Leia tucked back her hair. "Eric was opening his restaurant. Rebecca's family was investing. If she divorced him then, her parents would have pulled their funding. John and Trishelle, too. Add in the expense of a divorce where he was clearly at fault, and he would have gone under."

"But is that worth killing over? It's just a restaurant."

Leia quirked her head. "I know you'll eat anything, but do you do any fine dining?"

"Define *fine*."

"Food passed through a little abuelita's back window in El Salvador isn't what I'm talking about here. We do stories all the time in the Food section of our newspaper. If a high-profile chef doesn't succeed with a big restaurant project, it's over. A chef's reputation gets people in the door. Lose that and"—Leia made a slashing motion over her throat—"your career is over. You can't fail in any way."

Katherine felt sick. "So he had to get rid of Rebecca."

"If she died in a terrible accident—"

"Live. On TV. For everyone to see."

Leia nodded. "He'd have sympathy and support." It was brutal. Heartless. Stunningly efficient. "Nobody would suspect him." She shivered. Ice carving was dangerous, even in the best conditions. "He waited until Rebecca was under the sculpture. That's when he told Craig to make the cut."

He'd timed it perfectly.

"He killed her in cold blood," Katherine whispered.

"It's psychopathic," Leia declared. "She was his *wife*." She sat back, her face ashen. "And he's walking around free, here in the hotel with us."

Katherine was all too aware.

"And Roger knew." Leia's voice trembled. "He's been blackmailing Eric. That's why Eric's been in second place for four years. Roger didn't care about Rebecca—only winning. This guaranteed Eric stayed in second. Or else."

"But how? Eric can't control the judges or Roger's carving skill."

Silence fell between them. The ice walls seemed to close in.

The curtain fluttered.

Katherine gasped. She held her breath, straining to hear any sound from beyond the wisp of fabric.

"Just a sec," she whispered, wishing for more than a memorial book in her hand and a dying phone in her bra. She steeled herself. "Hello?" She whipped the curtain back.

The hallway was empty. Eerily silent.

Katherine surveyed the mishmash of snowy prints outside the door. Too many people had been up and down this hallway for her to know if anyone had been standing outside their door.

She smoothed the snow with her boot before dropping the curtain and returning to Leia. Now they'd know if anyone passed by their door. Or stopped outside. A fresh set of footprints would give them away.

"Who was it?" Leia asked, her attention lingering on the door.

"Nobody." She hoped. Katherine tossed the book onto the bed. "There's something I don't understand," she said, pacing despite the cold. "You saw the Icarus plans?"

"They were a mess. Like someone tossed them in the snow and stomped on them a few times."

"And that brown stain, like a burn mark. How did that happen when they were sealed in plastic?" Katherine flipped to the ballerina picture. "Roger supposedly designed this, but look at how the body is balanced." Precarious. Otherworldly. "What does it remind you of?"

"Icarus falling." Leia's hand flew to her chest. "Ohmygosh." The way the body stretched out in the arabesque, it was the same composition as Icarus and his falling wings, the same basic geometric structure as the scales that had crushed Rebecca.

"Eric, with his engineering background," Katherine said flatly. "He creates sculptures that defy gravity."

"You think he gave his designs to Roger every year?" Leia flushed. "That's why Roger was so weird about his plans, why his team couldn't talk to the others."

"If anyone who worked with Eric saw Roger's plans, they'd recognize Eric's style instantly."

"And know Roger never wrote them."

Katherine stopped pacing. "That's why Roger was cagey with John at the party. John asked about his plans for this year's competition, but Roger wouldn't tell him, even though he liked to brag. And Roger's team had no idea what they were supposed to do, because Roger didn't know yet! He had to get the plans from Eric first."

"And remember Paul at the cocoa stand?" Leia was practically vibrating on the bed. "John had a list of drink orders from Eric. Then Paul picked it up and asked if Roger had returned."

"Oh, my gosh. Paul thought Eric's handwriting was Roger's." Katherine settled onto the bed. "But something's off about Tuesday night. If you're getting blackmailed plans, why drink? And wouldn't it be suspicious for Eric to suddenly act friendly? Plus, sending Roger off drunk—that's leaving too much to chance. He couldn't plan on him wrecking his car."

Leia adjusted her position. "Maybe Eric drove with Roger passed out in the passenger seat and bailed before the car went over the edge."

"Then we'd have seen blood on the passenger seat, not the driver's. And why only on the seat? Not on the wheel or the dash?"

"I take it that's unusual for a crash?"

Images of twisted metal and shattered glass flashed through Katherine's mind. "Crashes are messy." She'd seen her fair share.

"Maybe Eric stabbed Roger with an icicle, but it melted before anyone could find the murder weapon."

Katherine laughed despite herself. "That's what everyone and their brother suggests when I tell them I'm thinking about writing a mystery novel."

"You are?" Leia asked, warming her hands by rubbing them together.

"Maybe." How hard could it be? "The trouble right now is that we can't prove anything." Therefore, they wouldn't be able to do anything about it. There would be no justice for Rebecca and no closure for the people who loved her.

"Maybe we're overlooking something." Leia reached for her notebook again.

Katherine's gaze drifted to the oasis scene, with its palm trees and the trio of yellow lights hovering over the desert sands.

"What is it?"

She must have been staring. "This wall." Katherine settled her heels into her boots. "It's so stark compared to everything else."

Leia shifted for a better look. "Those lights are just floating there. I'd have put blue lights in the water, not yellow ones hovering over sand dunes like UFOs." She straightened. "Something's missing."

In a blink, Katherine's mind went from zero to eureka!

Triangles.

Roger had sculpted this room. Where were the triangles?

Katherine's heart raced. "I think our answer lies in the pyramids."

Leia shot her a quizzical look. "There aren't any pyramids."

"Exactly." Katherine nodded, her voice tight. "They're missing."

## CHAPTER
# EIGHTEEN

Leia scrambled off the bed, boots half on for a closer look at the oasis. How had she missed it? "Roger, who included triangles in every room he designed, would never pass up the chance to carve the most famous triangles on Earth."

Kat joined her, squinting. "They should've been the centerpiece, right behind those dunes with the oasis reflecting them."

"Maybe Roger wasn't done. Like with Amy's room." Leia's gloved fingers hovered near the wall as if she could grasp the answer.

"It's possible." Kat draped her sleeping bag over her shoulders like an enormous shawl. "Here. Get in. It's freezing."

Leia hardly registered the cold as her mind churned. "Roger left the party to meet Eric for the plans. It would have to be someplace secluded. Someplace nearby. Everyone else was in the main lodge for the party."

Kat's eyes widened. "The empty ice hotel."

Leia's attention snapped to the curtained doorway. "Follow me."

She darted into the blue-lit hallway. The sphinx loomed nearby, witness to her earlier tumble. Beyond that lay the workshop—a treasure trove of murder weapons, not a lock in sight.

Kat burst out behind her, cursing at their boot prints before swiping them away.

"This is it." Leia's stomach churned. "Roger died right here. That hole I tripped in—The only way it could have formed is if someone dug a hole in the floor after the hotel was completed." She turned to Kat. "There's only one reason to dig up the floor and that's if there's an enormous bloody mess to clean up."

Kat took a second to process. Her gaze darted down the hall to the now-solid snow floor where the ghostly swipe of fingers across the sphinx's shoulder used to be.

Now they were erased.

Just like Roger.

Kat's voice caught. "You think they met in our room?"

"Maybe. Or he was fleeing. Picture it. They exchange plans. Roger leaves to finish his room. Something happens. Eric snaps, grabs a tool from the workshop and—" She mimed a wild swing, nearly clipping the sphinx's nose. "Roger dies here. Eric cleans up. The plans fall, get wet and bloody. The ink runs. It all fits."

In a horrific, terrible way.

Kat blinked twice at Leia and the scene she'd painted.

Right in the middle of the hallway.

Goosebumps prickled Leia's skin.

"I think you're right," Kat whispered, "but I really don't want you to be."

"Me neither."

## CHAPTER EIGHTEEN

A muffled thud echoed down the hall. They froze, ears straining in the sudden silence.

"Back to the room," Kat hissed, leading the way through the curtain.

As if that would keep them safe.

Leia retreated to the oasis wall while Kat scribbled her boot over their tracks before swishing the curtain closed. "We need to be quiet," she said, joining Leia. "And if Eric killed Roger in the hall, how'd he get him into the car?"

"Maybe an ATV." Leia's teeth chattered.

"With an open back? It'd be hard to load a body onto a luggage rack and drive through a resort full of people and security cameras." Kat draped her makeshift shawl over Leia's shoulders. "And then you'd have a bloody ATV to deal with."

Leia stiffened and lost the blanket. "What if the blood on the car seat was melted snow?" She spun toward the door. "The bloody snow from the hall, melted and poured into the car."

Kat blinked once. Twice. "That's…possible."

It was so very possible.

They exchanged a loaded look.

"You said crashes are messy. There should have been blood on the wheel. And on the airbags."

"The airbags didn't go off." Kat brought a hand to her head. "They don't deploy if no one's in the seat." She dropped her hand and stared at Leia. "The car was empty when it hit."

"So where is Roger?"

The question hung between them.

Leia blew into her hands and turned back to the carving of the oasis. "This is bugging me, too."

"A lot of things are bugging me."

Leia studied the carving, her nose nearly touching the ice. The cross-hatching on the fronds was unmistakable—a perfect match for Icarus's feathered wings. An artistic signature as damning as a fingerprint.

"Kat." Leia took a sharp step back pointing at the feather-fronds. "I don't think Roger ever left this room."

Kat's breath caught. "Eric carved this wall. It was a rushed job. That's why it's sparse."

"And after years of triangle torture, he erased the pyramids." Leia's throat went dry. Her gaze swept over the wall, landing between the fronds. "That space is large enough for a person to fit through."

"Or in," Kat said flatly.

Leia's pulse raced. "The wall's thick enough. No one would know."

Kat nodded grimly. "Come spring, bulldozers flatten everything. Roger's body would be crushed, buried."

"Or mangled beyond recognition." Leia's mind raced. "It would give Eric months to vanish while the police search a frozen lake."

Leia stumbled back until her thighs hit the bed.

Kat donned her coat. "Want to see if we're right?"

*Oh no! No, no, no, no, no!*

"We can't hack at the wall. We can't afford it. We signed a damage waiver. And we might find a dead body!"

One reason was enough, and they had three.

"If we don't, Eric walks," Kat said, zipping up her coat.

Leia felt suddenly hot. Way too hot. "I usually love your practical nature, but—"

Kat jabbed a finger at the wall. "That body is our only proof."

"If it's there." This was too much. "We could be wrong about everything."

"There's only one way to find out." Kat turned back to the wall.

Leia's head went light. She was going to faint. Right there.

"You're *not* going to faint."

"How did you know what I was thinking?" she snapped. She pressed a hand to her forehead.

She was burning up.

Maybe she was going to have a heart attack and then faint.

"Then what do you suggest we do?" Kat asked.

Leia swallowed hard. "We could go to the police."

"And tell them what? To dig into the wall? That missing pyramids mean murder?" Kat shook her head. "They'd never buy it. Not without proof. They're focused on the car. It's the only evidence. Meanwhile, only one thing can prove exactly what happened to Roger."

His body buried in the wall.

"If we dig and find nothing, Eric will know we're onto him." Leia's stomach churned. That wasn't just dangerous; it could ruin everything. "He could cover his tracks."

"What other choice do we have?" Kat asked, ever the pragmatist.

*Think.* "What about the front desk?"

"They'd decide we were nuts and ship us off to the spa again."

"Dang it." Kat was right. Leia weighed her options. Dig a hole. Forfeit their deposit. Find a body and possibly enrage the killer who could be lurking right beyond their flimsy curtain of a door.

Or...

Do nothing. Let him escape. Find a cozy hotel with a

proper lock, preferably a deadbolt. Return to her lovely, cozy home and pretend none of this ever happened.

She had to admit it was tempting. Familiar.

And much, much safer.

"Hey," Kat said gently. "If you don't want to do this, we won't."

Leia felt her shoulders ease. "I appreciate that." Kat would never force her. She'd never been that type of friend. Leia took a deep breath. Thankfully, they were in this together, right or wrong.

But could she simply walk away? Would she be a person who ignored the truth, who failed to bring justice to someone who needed it?

Leia studied the palm trees, the lights, the empty space where the pyramids should be. "If we're wrong about this—"

"We're not," Kat vowed.

That was almost worse. "If we're right—"

"Then we help catch a killer." Kat drew close. "We give justice to Rebecca, closure to her family and friends. We make it as right as it can be."

Leia wiped the beaded sweat from her upper lip and tugged her gloves tight. "Let's do it."

## CHAPTER
# NINETEEN

Katherine surveyed the wall, doubt gnawing at her resolve. She worked her fingers deeper into her gloves. Beside her, Leia fidgeted like a boxer awaiting the bell, her face about five shades too pale. Hopefully just the lighting.

"Care to do the honors?" Leia's voice wavered.

Not particularly. But as with everything in life, Katherine did what needed doing. "Say goodbye to the security deposit." She balled her fist.

"Good thing I've got a steady paycheck," Leia said, taking her position.

Leia's hand darted toward the wall, then retreated. Once. Twice. Three times.

Katherine braced and struck. Right through the oasis. The impact jolted her arm, ice fracturing beneath her knuckles.

Leia yelped. Katherine pried out a frozen chunk.

"Oh, geez." Leia took a forceful swing of her own.

"Stay low. Roger's body would be heavy. Eric likely

made an opening near the ground." She scraped at the wall, but the snow was dense, possibly refrozen from body heat.

"Right, smart." Leia nodded, scratching like a frantic squirrel. "You're disturbingly good at this murder stuff."

Katherine merely shrugged, attacking the unyielding wall. It was too icy. "This isn't working." They'd hardly made a dent. Anxiety clawed at her. "Maybe we're wrong. Eric couldn't dig a body-sized hole unnoticed."

Leia stepped back. "He'd need all night. Unless he used a chainsaw."

A spark of inspiration hit Katherine. "Leia, you're a genius!" She dashed for the door. "Come on."

"Oh, fantastic. We're adding chainsaw theft to our list of crimes tonight." Leia hurried after her. "I can't believe we're doing this!"

"Neither can I. But not a chainsaw. Something less noisy."

"Oh, well, that makes it all better," Leia said as they crept down the empty hall as fast as they could go.

No doubt they'd find plenty of options waiting to be borrowed from the workshop.

"Too late to turn back now," Katherine murmured, her legs unsteady as they passed yet another curtained room.

The corridor was deserted, offering plenty of dark, quiet rooms for someone to hide in.

"Just think, the killer probably did this exact thing." Leia wrestled with the chain across the door.

"I'm trying not to dwell on that," Katherine said, stepping over it.

"Right." Leia followed suit, entering the shadowy workshop.

"There." Katherine pointed to a row of ice chisels on the pegboard. "Those will work nicely."

## CHAPTER NINETEEN

Leia locked in on the chisel with the dented tip. "I'm taking that one, too."

They each grabbed an ice chisel to dig with as well. Katherine tucked a mallet into the loop on her pajama pants. Always prepared. "Ready?"

Leia held the dented chisel with two gloved fingers. "As I'll ever be."

They clutched their tools and hurried back.

"In hindsight, I think I could use another spa day," Leia muttered, pushing through their curtain. She deposited the dented chisel on the bed next to her notebook.

Katherine surveyed the room to make sure they were alone.

Leia examined the minimal damage they'd inflicted on the ice wall. "We might be able to patch this up."

"Too late now." Katherine swung the mallet, driving her chisel deep.

Leia flinched. "I didn't like my deposit anyway," she said, plunging her chisel into the center.

No hiding it now.

The chisels worked wonders, leveraging out large chunks. Their small hole grew into a tunnel, forcing them to reach deeper.

Hack. Sweep. Hack. A lightbulb swayed. Hack. Each strike felt like a desecration, ice and snow flying as they excavated.

Katherine's muscles burned, her core screaming as she reached into the growing cavern. Knots built in her neck and shoulders, but she pressed on.

Snow piled around their feet in growing mounds.

"Any chance we can claim this was an accident?" Leia panted, the sound of their labored breathing and the scrape of metal on ice filling the tomb-like room.

"Not unless you can blame a rabid badger," Katherine groaned. "Or a polar bear." The hole was nearly den-sized.

Suddenly, her chisel caught on something. The end snagged in fabric. She stumbled back.

Dropping the tool, she dug with her hands, careful not to damage evidence. Leia joined in. She brushed snow from something knitted and bright red.

A large chunk gave way with a soft thud.

"Leia," she gasped, transfixed.

Protruding from the freshly carved hole was a human hand, frozen solid, fingers curled as if reaching out from its icy tomb.

## CHAPTER
# TWENTY

Leia's scream died in her throat, muffled by her gloved hands. Her lungs ached with the effort to hold it back. Cold sweat trickled down her neck as she stared at the horrifying revelation. "That's a hand, Kat. That's a hand."

Kat panted, brushing snow off the pale, lifeless fingers. Their tips were yellowish, the palm a mottled purple. "It looks like we found the Ice King."

"How do you know it's Roger?" Leia kicked herself mentally. Of course it was Roger. It wasn't like there was another scheming, blackmailing ice sculptor around who'd gone missing recently.

"See the discoloration?" Kat explained as if she were back at the hospital and not in a room in a remote ice hotel. Staring at a dead guy. "That's Reynaud's phenomenon. Fairly common in heavy smokers. Roger wasn't here long before he died. His fingertips would've turned blue from lack of oxygen if he'd been out in the cold. Proves he only came to meet Eric, not to work on the room, and he died quickly."

"Okay, but how do we prove Eric killed him?" Leia forced herself to look at the hand again.

"Good point." Kat gripped her chisel and slammed it into the wall near the hand.

Leia's stomach flipped. "You're going to dig him out entirely?" She could handle a hand. Maybe. But the rest?

"I'm not going for Roger," Kat grunted, taking another whack. And another. "Look closer. Under the ice."

Red knit fabric.

Leia wasn't sure what it meant until Katherine pulled a knit toque from the icy tomb, its bright crimson marred by a splatter of dark bloodstains.

Her fingers shook so hard she nearly dropped it. But she kept her grip and her cool and held up the bloody toque. "Here's our evidence."

Leia gasped, then rushed to retrieve the memorial photo book. "Here's more proof." She flipped to Eric's smiling face. "I've only seen one of these, and it was on Eric's head."

Kat looked from the book to the hat. The blood, the glittering snow, the embroidered *Flambé* logo. "Case closed." She dropped it on the pile like it had stung her.

Leia's breath went shallow. "We need to get the police. Now."

"Right." Kat fished her phone from her bra, then cursed. "The battery's dead."

Leia retrieved hers from her pants. She had juice, but no signal. "I can't call!"

"Take pictures," Kat urged. "Of the hand. The hat. Everything. Show the front desk. You can call the police from there."

Fighting nausea, Leia snapped a series of photos. "Okay,

# CHAPTER TWENTY

let's go." She started off but stopped when her friend stood firm in the piles of ice they had pulled from the wall.

"I should stay here," Kat said, resolute.

"Are you insane? There's a dead body right there!"

"I'm used to that," Kat reasoned.

"There's evidence that could put a killer away for life."

"I'll guard it," Kat vowed. When Leia hesitated, she added, "We need to keep everything together in the room. We've already disturbed the crime scene enough."

"You're not wrong," Leia said, "but I still don't like it."

"I don't, either," Kat said grimly. "But if Eric's prowling around, he might move the body while we're arguing with the police."

"Which is exactly why you shouldn't be here alone. He's a killer, Kat."

"I know." Kat squared her shoulders. "But our only shot at catching him is if he thinks his secret's safe. If he suspects anything, he'll take off. Me being here will force the hotel and the police to act fast. If we're both in the lobby, they'll waste hours interrogating us before checking this out."

Leia's stomach twisted. "I can't leave you here."

"I'll be fine. Watch." Kat tucked herself into her sleeping bag, feigning loud snores. "Anyone passing will think we're fast asleep, not babysitting a corpse. They won't have any reason to poke around."

Except for the large hole in the wall.

But Leia knew when she could budge Kat and when she couldn't. And in this case, she had to trust her friend to get out of there if she needed to.

Leia handed her a chisel. "Keep this with you, just in case."

"Watch your back out there. I'm not the only one taking a chance."

Leia looked down at her friend, wild haired and bundled in her sleeping bag, and felt a surge of affection. "I never meant for this when I said we should go on an adventure." She wrapped Kat in a fierce hug.

Kat was like a sister to her. If anything happened to her in there after Leia had asked her to come—

"Quick," Kat urged, gripping the chisel. "Before your battery dies and you can't show them the pictures."

Leia bolted from the room, then caught herself. Running looked suspicious. She slowed to a hurried walk only to realize she'd turned the wrong way. The ice halls felt like a maze, surreal blue light making everything feel colder, stranger.

Phantom footsteps dogged her. She whirled, staring down the empty corridor behind her.

"Get ahold of yourself," she whispered.

If Kat could sit with a dead body, she could do this.

Still, her heart raced as she neared a blind corner in the hall.

She forced her way forward and saw a glowing red Exit sign.

Hallelujah! She burst into the frigid night. She had to get help. Safety. Panic drove her toward the cabins for a brief second before she remembered she was headed for the front desk.

She pivoted and slammed straight into Eric as he loaded duffel bags onto an ATV.

He appeared shocked and not at all happy to see her. She managed a semblance of a smile. "Hey."

"What are you doing out here?" He abandoned his task. "Leia, right?"

Her heart sped up.

Did he know?

*He knew.*

He was packing up. Escaping in the dead of night.

She backed toward the hotel. "Oh, you know. Couldn't sleep." She eyed the lodge. Safety. It was too far to call for help. "Thought I would take a quick walk." She tried to make her tone chipper but failed. She'd never make it.

He tilted his head, his smile vanishing. "It's not even dawn."

Leia's cheeks flushed. "Oh, good. I love an early morning walk. You too?" she asked, despite the obvious.

"Loading up the truck," he said, watching her carefully. "I'm heading out right after the awards ceremony. It's a long drive back to Texas."

And the border, Leia realized. Even shorter if he drove north.

They were running out of time.

Eric's eyes narrowed. "You look nervous. Is something wrong?"

Leia's breath quickened. "Oh, no. Only tired. Maybe I should forget the walk and head back to the cabin. Get a little rest before the celebration."

"The cabins are that way." He pointed in the opposite direction as she backed toward the lodge. He strode after her, his pace quickening as hers did. "What's going on? Where's your friend?"

"Look, she snores, okay?" Leia blurted, louder than she'd intended. "I haven't slept all night. Then I kept imagining the snow ceiling collapsing on us. I'm at my wit's end!"

Eric raised his hands. "Fair enough." His voice dropped to a different register entirely. "Hey—" He lunged forward, closing the distance between them in one fluid motion.

She dodged away from his grasp.

Her phone buzzed. She whipped it out, nearly tossing it, hitting the Answer button instead. A green-feathered face filled the screen.

"Hiiiiiiiiiiii!" Charley's parroty voice cut through the dark. "You up to somethin'?"

Eric froze, his expression shifting as he realized she wasn't alone anymore.

She was dead if he realized she was talking to a bird.

"Call from home. Gotta go!" The words tumbled out as she held the phone to her chest and hurried for the lodge, trying not to run.

Afraid he'd chase.

*Thank you, Charley.*
*Thank you, Charley.*
*Thank you, Charley.*

"We're not done here." Eric's voice had gone flat, almost pleasant.

That was worse somehow.

She risked a glance over her shoulder. He stood unnaturally still, jaw clenched.

That was it. She gave in to a dead sprint.

As she ran, a horrifying thought struck her. Had she just put Kat in danger? She slowed her pace, nearly tripping over her own boots.

Should she go back?

If she did, they might both be trapped with a killer with no one to save them.

She looked over her shoulder. Eric was staring after her, his frame tense. Then, to her horror, he turned and began walking toward the ice hotel.

*Oh, no, no, no, no.*
She had to get help. Fast.

## CHAPTER
# TWENTY-ONE

Katherine huddled in her sleeping bag, her throat raw from exaggerated snores. Each second stretched into eternity.

She'd warmed quickly but still shivered, her eyes fixed on the curtain.

Not on the body in the wall.

She hoped Leia was okay.

And that she hadn't run into Eric.

Alone.

He'd see through Leia in a second, and she had no doubt he'd kill again to keep his secret.

She clutched the chisel until her knuckles ached.

*What were they thinking?* They never should have started this.

Leia was taking too long.

Katherine squeezed her eyes shut, trying to think positive. Leia had run track. She could get help fast.

But if that was the case, why wasn't she back yet?

She stared at the flimsy blue curtain shielding her.

Before, it had been fun to be the only people left in their

section. Like they were the brave ones. The last ones standing.

Now?

The hallway lay eerily silent.

It felt like she could scream and scream and no one would ever know.

For one brief, insane moment, she considered flipping on the lights and music, if only to break the oppressive stillness.

Leia definitely should have been back by now. Something was wrong.

She should have gone with her friend. After all, she didn't have many. Just coworkers. A knot formed in her stomach. She didn't know what she'd do if something terrible happened to Leia.

A *thunk* echoed from the empty room next door. Or maybe from the hallway.

She stiffened, straining to listen.

*Please don't let it be Eric.* Making sure she wasn't poking into things she shouldn't.

Like the wall.

Her breath went shallow. Sure, she had a weapon, but she was no match for a killer.

She'd tried to smooth the snow in front of the doorway every time they entered. That way, she'd know if someone had been outside. Listening.

Waiting.

But it hadn't gone very well. Both she and Leia had run across the smooth snow at least once without thinking. She'd tried again anyway.

She curled up tighter.

She wouldn't survive five minutes in one of her mystery novels.

# CHAPTER TWENTY-ONE

Her hand had gone numb around the chisel. She switched it to her left hand and shook out her right as hushed footsteps whispered down the hall, directly toward her.

She fought the urge to bolt upright.

*Please be someone with a weak bladder and no fear of the port-a-potty at the end of the hall.*

And, oh no—she'd completely forgotten to snore!

She let out a loud snurfle, doing her best impression of a congested walrus. Her heart hammered against her ribs.

The boots halted.

Katherine kept at it, letting out a choking snore that would make a grizzly proud. *That's right, big guy. Keep walking. Nothing to see here but a hibernating bear with a deadly chisel.*

She'd slept in disaster zones but never felt this exposed.

Another snore, this one morphing into a whimper, her heart heavy and her raw throat ready to give out.

In between snores, she strained to listen past the curtain.

Silence in the hall.

She drew a sharp breath. She didn't dare move.

This was her job. Stay put. Play possum. Keep the evidence safe.

Her mind drifted to Leia. In spite of all of this, she'd do it again in a heartbeat. If they made it through, she promised herself she'd make more room in her life for fun.

It was silly, really.

Except that it wasn't.

The curtain swayed, and she barely stifled a yelp as she passed the chisel back to her right hand, gripping it hard.

❋

Leia resisted the urge to vault over the stone fireplace, to karate chop the antler lamps, to do *something*, even if it was to bang her head on the polished wood of the lobby reception desk at the lodge. "I'm telling you. We need the police. Now."

The night clerk looked like she was working her first job that didn't involve babysitting her cousins. "I'm doing the best I can, ma'am." Her voice quivered as she clutched a training manual, her crisp blue uniform a stark contrast to the sweat dripping down Leia's back. "You saw me place the call. They'll be on their way soon. Would you like a cookie?" She tilted her head toward a tray at the far end of the desk.

Leia's face burned, her hands balling into fists. "No, I don't want a cookie. I want a homicide investigation team."

"We have oatmeal raisin," the clerk added helplessly.

Leia inhaled deep and tried to channel her inner Buddha. Which was difficult when all she wanted to do was climb over the desk, grab the phone, and call every CSI team within a thousand-mile radius.

Instead, she forced a smile. "I don't think you're listening to what I'm saying."

The clerk swiped at the frazzled halo of hair that had escaped her ponytail and snuck a peek at the manual. "I have done everything I can to address the patron's... I'm sorry. I have done my best to address your needs in a calm and cheerful manner." She abandoned the book. "Look, it's crazy early morning. Our local force is small. We can't do anything until they get here." A horrified expression crossed her features before she wiped it clean and straightened her jacket. "We have to be patient," she snipped, her voice an octave higher than it should have been.

"We don't have time to be patient," Leia said through

## CHAPTER TWENTY-ONE

clenched teeth. "I'm telling you Eric Hardney is a killer. The body of his latest victim is In. My. Room." She shoved a hand down her shirt. "I have pictures!" She fished out her phone, tapped the home screen, and realized it was dead. A brick. A useless lump when she needed it most. "Okay, I can't show you now."

"Please don't," the clerk pleaded, accidentally knocking her manual onto the floor. "I promise it'll be okay."

Leia slammed her hand down onto the desk. "Eric is packing to leave. My friend might be in trouble. We don't have time to stand around. Where's hotel security?"

Her lower lip trembled. "There was an incident tonight with a dangerous animal near the lodge. They're scaring it off. They'll be back soon."

"Was it a moose?" Leia asked. What was she doing?! "Where's the manager?"

The clerk's doe-like eyes widened. "I am the manager. In training. At night. Part-time. Actually, my training starts next week."

"Call the real one."

"I did," she insisted. "I tried," she pleaded. "It went to voicemail."

Leia couldn't take it. Kat was alone, guarding evidence of a murder. And the last she'd seen, the killer had been headed that way.

She needed to get back.

"Tell the police I'll be in my room with the evidence."

Without waiting for a response, she bolted for the door. The frigid air slapped her in the face as she sprinted across the snow-covered expanse between the lodge and the ice hotel.

Eric's ATV sat abandoned.

There was no sign of him.

She picked up the pace.

The side entrance loomed before her, a gaping maw shielded by strips of plastic insulation. Leia slipped inside, her boots crunching on the snow.

The dim light in the halls cast shadows that danced and shifted with each step. The air hung heavy, each breath visible in small, panicked puffs.

Eric could be anywhere.

She pressed forward and made a right down the hall toward her room. And as she turned the corner, she heard a faint clicking sound.

Leia froze.

It was coming from the workshop.

She kept her steps slow, light, willing them to be silent as she neared the workshop and peeked inside.

Eric stood with his back to her, reaching for a tool on the wall. A rusty ice clamp. Those tongs were both sharp and heavy. If Roger had been hit in the head with those, he hadn't stood a chance. Leia's stomach clenched. Eric hefted it in his hand, then dropped it into a bucket with a dull thud.

*The* bucket he'd used to collect the bloody snow he planted in Roger's car?

It had to be.

Leia ducked back as he turned. She pressed against the icy wall, praying he hadn't seen her. The clink of metal tongs against the bucket told her he was on the move.

Drawing closer.

She closed her eyes.

Silence. He'd stopped.

Leia swallowed hard and ventured a quick glance inside. Eric had bent to tie his boot.

She dashed past the workshop entrance and hurried

## CHAPTER TWENTY-ONE

down the hall as quickly as she could without making a sound. She barely wanted her feet to touch snow. If she could, she would have stopped breathing entirely as she rushed for her room and Kat.

Leia burst through the swept snow in the doorway, through the curtain.

"Kat!" she hissed.

Kat lay on the bed, motionless. A wave of panic seized her. "Kat!"

Kat rolled over, eyes widening. "Leia, I'm so glad to see you!"

Leia rushed to her, enveloping her in a tight hug. "Me too. I was so worried."

Kat pulled away. "Are the police coming?"

"Yes." Leia nodded. "Soon, I hope." She ran a hand through her hair. "Evidently, they're a small force and not at all close by."

Kat gaped at her. "Did you tell them about the hand sticking out of the wall?"

"I did." Leia paced the small room. "They've got to be here soon. We have a body. We have Eric's hat." Her voice dropped. "I saw Eric in the workshop just now."

Kat about fell over. "He's here?"

Leia nodded, her attention darting to the door. "He's making off with a bucket and one of those big ice clamps."

"He's taking the tools he used to kill Roger," Kat said breathlessly. "He's just going to walk out the door with the evidence."

Leia gave a curt nod. "He doesn't know we have the hat," she said, returning to Kat on the bed.

Kat tensed. "Do you think he'll come for it?"

"He wouldn't know we dug it out of the wall." Leia glanced to the hand, regretting it as soon as she did. "I tried to show the clerk my pictures, but my phone died." She drew it from her coat pocket.

Kat nodded sharply. "Was the snow outside the door clear when you walked in?"

"I think so." Leia's head went light. "I don't know. I was running."

"Did you wipe your prints?" Kat pressed, pushing out of her sleeping bag.

"No." She'd been thinking about Kat. "I'll do it."

"I'll fix it." Kat swung her legs off the bed.

"I'm good," Leia insisted, beating her to the door. She whipped open the curtain.

Eric stood on the other side, an ice pick in hand.

Kat let out a strangled cry. The air froze in Leia's lungs.

Eric's face twisted in a mix of regret and dangerous determination. He slowly shook his head. "You made a big mistake."

# CHAPTER
# TWENTY-TWO

Eric strolled into the room, the ice pick dangling casually at his side. In his other hand, he swung the utility bucket with the rusted ice tongs. His eyes glinted like a predator cornering its prey. "Just couldn't leave things alone, could you?"

Leia's voice trembled. "This was a mistake." Coming here. Staying here. Digging into the wall. "Please don't hurt us."

Eric's face remained impassive. "I think you owe me a hat."

His gaze swept the room, barely noting the hand emerging from the icy wall, settling on the red toque crumpled on the pile of snow.

He used the ice pick to lift it. "Much obliged," he said, dropping it into the bucket.

Kat inched toward the bed. Leia silently willed her to stop.

"You killed Roger." Kat's voice cracked. "You buried him in the wall."

Eric closed the distance between them. "I killed Roger,"

he said, his tone eerily casual. He pressed the tip of the ice pick against Kat's chest. "But I'm not a killer."

What the—"That's your hat," Leia blurted.

Eric turned to her, his gaze piercing. "What was I supposed to do?" He clutched the ice pick so hard his knuckles turned white. "Roger had been humiliating me for the last four years. Do you know what that feels like?"

"Um—" Leia's mind raced, searching for words.

Eric paced, gesticulating wildly with the ice pick. "Then he demands more. He wants the *perfect* sculpture. What does that even mean?" His free hand raked through his hair. "He won every year, and it still wasn't enough. It was never going to be enough."

"Enough to make up for killing Rebecca?" Leia seethed, the words escaping before she could think.

"What?" Eric spat.

She flinched and retreated, her back to the wall.

"I didn't want to kill her," Eric said, almost to himself. He gestured helplessly with his ice pick. "Amy discovered I was married at the worst possible time. I didn't know she'd signed up for the Jack Oak competition. I'd steered her away from events Rebecca and I did together."

"What a gentleman," Leia bit out.

"Are you done?" he growled.

As long as he had that ice pick pointed at her, she was.

"It wasn't like that," he said, lowering the weapon slightly. "Amy decided to surprise me by entering her first large competition." He huffed. "When she met my wife, she flipped out. I tried to explain, but of course she didn't listen. Instead, she told Rebecca *everything*." He swore. "I was so deep in debt from Flambé, and a divorce would have ruined me." He shook his head. "I convinced Rebecca to keep quiet until we could get counseling, but you didn't know

# CHAPTER TWENTY-TWO

Rebecca. She was proud, and she could never keep anything to herself. She made it clear she didn't blame little clueless Amy. She blamed me."

"So you engineered the accident," Kat said, her voice calm. Only her eyes betrayed her panic.

Eric sighed, and Leia could have sworn she saw regret in his eyes. For himself or for what he'd done to Rebecca?

He adjusted his grip on the ice pick. "A stupid affair shouldn't destroy a man's life. Amy was just a foolish twenty-two-year-old I coached at an up-and-comers' event in New England. I didn't think she'd ever find out about my wife, much less give Rebecca everything she needed to bankrupt me. It wasn't fair for me to lose everything over one mistake."

Leia felt sick. His victims' lives meant nothing to him. Rebecca, Roger...he'd killed them for his ambitions. And Amy? He'd used her without thinking twice and probably encouraged her guilt over the accident to keep her quiet.

He pointed the ice pick at Leia. "Your phone, please."

With shaking fingers, she handed it over.

He pulled a portable charger from his pocket, connected the phone, and tossed both in the bucket.

"That was the first body I've had to bury. When I realized my hat was gone, probably in there with poor Roger, well..." He gritted his teeth. "You can imagine how upsetting that was."

He loomed over her. Leia felt the urge to run, but he'd be faster.

He lifted the tongs from the bucket, studying them like artwork. "Funny how fast a man can die." He touched the blunt tip to Leia's head. "Bam. Then it's not my problem anymore as long as no one finds out."

She drew a sharp breath.

"Cut it out," Kat snapped.

Eric shot her a long look. "I don't think you're in a position to give orders."

"It's okay," Leia managed.

Spoiler alert: it wasn't.

Eric smirked. "I was going to have to flee the country, go somewhere without extradition." He wrinkled his nose and dropped the tongs back into the bucket. "Talk about a change in lifestyle. But what else could I do?" He wrapped an arm around Leia's shoulders. "Now that you've located my property for me, I can have my old life back." He squeezed hard enough to hurt. "Thank you."

"If you try to kill us, we'll fight back hard." Kat's voice faltered. "I know where the jugular is."

"If I killed you, where would I put you?" Eric drawled. "The hotel's all done."

Leia's jaw clenched, her hands balling into fists.

Eric pulled away and held out the bucket to her. "Your phone should boot back up. You're going to erase those pictures while I watch."

Leia's arm felt stiff as she reached into the bucket that had held Roger's blood. She fished her phone from atop the bloody red toque.

Hopefully, it would still be a brick.

"Do it," Eric ordered as she fired up the phone to one percent power. It hurt like a physical blow as she moved her fingers over the screen and deleted her pictures of the hat. Eric lifted the phone out of her hand to double-check her work. "No signal means no backup to the cloud. Sorry, girls."

Leia shared a deflated look with Kat.

He was right.

Eric's face hardened. "Spring would've made things

## CHAPTER TWENTY-TWO

harder to cover up. I had to leave the tongs and bucket in the workshop, hoping more fingerprints might muddle the evidence. But now thanks to you, there's nothing left to tie me to any of this."

He was forgetting something. Leia's gaze darted to the bent chisel on the bed.

Good.

Eric shot her a sly smile. "I never touched that. And Roger won't be needing it again."

He held up the bucket containing the ice clamp and his toque. "This'll be at the bottom of a lake before you can convince the police to go looking for it. And for as much as you can tell stories about an accident everyone saw with their own eyes, no one's going to believe a pair of nosy old women with no actual proof."

"Old?" Leia shot back.

Where *were* the police?

They had to keep him there, talking.

Kat seemed to be thinking the same thing.

"You just confessed," she pointed out.

Eric held out his hands. "Oh, I'm sorry. Are you law enforcement? Do you want to read me my rights." He tilted his head. "You have nothing but hearsay and speculation. Anyone could have killed Roger, and plenty wanted to. So what can you prove?"

Kat fell silent.

Eric's grin widened as he lifted the bucket. "Nothing without this." He swung it like he hadn't a care in the world as he strolled for the door. "Thanks again, ladies," he said, flicking the curtain closed behind him.

Leia felt a rush of panic. "He's going to get away with it."

They waited until his boots faded down the hall before

bolting in the opposite direction toward the ice-hotel lobby.

A laughing sun carved in the wall mocked their desperation as they ran. They burst through the empty bar and out through the lobby, the frigid air whipping their skin.

"This way," Leia said as they ran along the high snow walls, scanning for Eric until they reached the spot where his ATV had been.

"It's gone," Leia hissed. "We've got to get back to the front desk in the lodge. I'll call the police myself."

They sprinted across the snow, nearly colliding with Ian carrying a sleeping bag.

"Ian!" Kat stumbled to a stop. "Eric killed Roger. He's destroying the evidence right now."

"What?" Ian stared, slack-jawed. "Are you sure?"

Leia nodded frantically. "We need to stop him."

"I—" he began.

But they were already running. To the lodge, to the desk.

The clerk had her training manual open again. She looked up, clutching it like a shield. "Welcome to the Jack Oak—"

"Why aren't you doing anything?" Leia demanded, slamming her hands on the counter. "There's a murderer getting away!"

"He's killed twice!" Kat shrieked.

"You're upset." The clerk's hands fluttered to her manual. Leia reached behind the desk and grabbed the phone.

"Please don't—" The clerk's voice cracked. "Security might call—"

Just then Eric strolled by the front windows, the bucket swinging casually at his side.

"It's him!" Kat pointed.

"Right there." Leia couldn't believe it.

The clerk yanked the phone back. "I promise I'm trying —" When she looked up, Eric had vanished. "I don't see anyone."

Leia's head threatened to explode. "He is right outside!"

"And he's getting away," Kat wailed, pointing at the tall lodge doors.

The clerk's chin wobbled as she straightened her shoulders. "That is not a guest issue. That's for the police to handle when they arrive!"

Kat's face went red. "Sure. Let's wait until he's destroyed all the evidence."

The clerk flinched. "Would you like a spa voucher for your trouble?"

"No!" they shouted together.

Leia lost control of her hands completely, gesticulating wildly. "A body in the wall cannot be canceled by a spa voucher! There aren't enough hot stones or fountains or fluffy towels in the world to make this right!"

An engine rumbled outside.

They abandoned the clerk, who was now hyperventilating into her manual, and burst through the doors, their boots slipping on the icy steps. They stumbled to a halt, watching in horror as Eric nonchalantly brushed the snow off his windshield with his sleeve. They stood helplessly as he tossed the bucket into his pickup truck bed and climbed into the cab. He waved and flashed them a smug grin before slamming the door and pulling away.

CHAPTER

# TWENTY-THREE

The frigid air bit into Leia's lungs.

*He's escaping!*

Eric's taillights blazed crimson against the rising dawn as he turned toward the exit.

Her fingers curled into fists, a primal scream clawing at her throat.

"Once he hits that road, he's as good as gone," Kat hissed through clenched teeth.

Suddenly, a thunderous roar cut through the morning stillness.

Kat's hand shot out, nearly clotheslining her. "There!"

To their left, a familiar flatbed work truck burst from the employee lot on the west side, Ian at the helm. It barreled toward the main lot.

Hope surged.

Only the gate was closed. Locked. Completely blocking the access road for resort vehicles.

"What's his plan?" Kat started for the gate.

"He won't make it in time." Leia sprinted, gesturing wildly.

"Ian, the gate!" Kat shouted, her voice raw with sheer panic.

Ian's hand darted to the visor. He jabbed a remote, and the gate shuddered to life.

"Faster," Kat urged.

The gate twitched and began an agonizingly slow ascent.

"Move it, you glorified toothpick," Leia pleaded.

Eric hit the gas, his truck fishtailing to the left, kicking up a spray of snow, gunning for the far side of the lot.

Frick. "Eric's got a clear shot."

"Ian's not stopping." Kat pointed toward the advancing truck.

Worse, he hit the gas. The engine of the resort work truck roared. Sleeping bags cascaded from the back like multicolored confetti as Ian hurtled toward the half-open gate.

Leia's heart hammered against her ribs. "Go, Ian!"

Ian white-knuckled the wheel, his expression set in stone.

The gate exploded in a shower of splinters as Ian's truck plowed through, tires screaming as he wrenched the wheel.

Kat grabbed her arm. "He's racing Eric to the exit."

But Ian couldn't keep up the chase for long—not in that massive work truck. It was built for hauling, not speed.

Ian didn't seem to care.

Kat and Leia sprinted after them down the main aisle as the two trucks played an insane game of chicken.

Only one could win.

Ian smashed over a speed bump, and for a terrifying moment, the truck teetered. But he held his course, slamming sideways across the exit with a bone-jarring crunch. The sleeping bags flew like rice at a wedding.

## CHAPTER TWENTY-THREE

Eric plowed forward.

Ian braced for impact.

Eric slammed on the brakes. Too late.

"Oh my. Ian!" Kat cried.

Leia resisted the urge to shield her eyes as Eric's pickup screeched to a halt a hair's breadth from Ian's driver's side door.

Kat's jubilant cry pierced the air. "We've got him now!"

No, they didn't.

With a nauseating grind of tires on ice, Eric yanked his wheel. The pickup spun, kicking up a blinding spray of snow. When it cleared, they saw Eric's vehicle pointed toward the eastern tree line by the creek-side trailhead.

"What's he—" Leia's question died on her lips as Eric's engine roared to life.

Oh no.

Kat's expression fell. "He's going off-road."

A cold knot formed in the pit of Leia's stomach, her mouth going dry as she watched Eric's truck aim toward the tree line. "He's going to get away!"

After all they'd been through. After everything they'd done. He'd run. He'd escape. The police wouldn't launch a manhunt, not until they'd investigated the case themselves and grasped the true horror of Eric's crime. Not until they realized he'd murdered Rebecca and killed Roger, entombing him in ice. And they might never uncover the truth without the evidence he was running away with *right now*.

Kat's voice cut through her spiraling thoughts, steadying and certain. "No. Wait. This is it. We've got him now."

No, they didn't. And it was worse than before. At least

before they'd dug out the bloody toque, it had been there for police to find. Eventually.

Now? She didn't want to look.

"Leia, watch," Kat pressed.

"No. I—" *Oh my.*

A knowing look crossed Kat's features as Eric's pickup left the groomed lot on the verge of a clean getaway.

And he would have succeeded.

Except for one thing.

"I can't unsee it now," Leia said, hoping against hope it truly did span the entire length of the parking lot.

"It got me," Kat insisted, eyes on the truck.

*Loose powder.*

Every detail etched itself into Leia's mind with crystal clarity—the arc of snow spraying from Eric's tires, the glint of sunrise on his windshield. His whoop of victory, the tilt of his truck as it crested a small rise in the snow-covered ground.

*Please be there, please be there, please be there.*

For an instant, Eric's truck soared over the rise, silhouetted against the fiery northern dawn, a picture of triumphant escape.

Then it happened.

The truck's front end plummeted as if the earth had opened its maw to swallow it. A thunderous crunch echoed across the lot as the vehicle nose-dived into an invisible trap.

"The drainage ditch," Kat said with a wealth of satisfaction.

"Gets you every time." Leia crossed her arms.

The front end of the pickup was buried, its rear wheels spinning uselessly in the air like an upended beetle.

Sirens wailed, cutting through the eerie stillness of

dawn, growing louder as a procession of police vehicles swung into the resort. Their lights painted the snow in alternating washes of red and blue. Ian maneuvered the battered resort truck out of the way. The cavalry had arrived, and this time, they had their work cut out for them.

Deputies surrounded the half-sunken pickup. The bucket, tongs, and hat lay scattered on the pristine snow, a damning array of evidence.

Leia threw her arm over Kat's shoulder, giddy to the bone. They watched a dazed and defeated Eric stumble from the driver's side and collapse into the powder. He blinked in disbelief, hands raised above his head with a mix of shock and resignation.

"We did it," Leia said. "We really did it."

Kat nodded, leaning into her friend. "We make a pretty good team."

"Always did," Leia said, bumping Kat's hip with her own.

The dawn wind swirled around them, but Leia had never felt warmer. The chase was over. The killer was caught. And they only had one thing left to do.

## CHAPTER
# TWENTY-FOUR

Katherine practiced her deep breathing, drawing in the fragrant steam of her mocha before taking a sip. The warmth of the morning sun lent comfort, even as she kept her eyes closed against the early brightness. The bonfire's heat danced across her skin, a stark contrast to the crisp morning air.

Leia kept watch beside her on the bench, her friend's restless foot sending tiny tremors through the wood.

"I didn't think this would be so hard," Leia said, rubbing her gloves against the smooth grain. "I know I wanted more than anything to set things right, but—oh jeez, here they come."

Katherine's eyes fluttered open. She took a fortifying sip of her mocha, channeling the composure she'd observed in countless doctors before they delivered life-altering news. She'd always been grateful the burden hadn't fallen on her shoulders.

But now, she'd do her best.

John and Trishelle's laughter pierced the morning stillness. They strolled hand in hand like high school sweethearts.

"Hey!" John called out. "Our favorite new ice enthusiasts!"

Katherine raised her mug. "Come join us."

They settled onto the bench kitty-corner to Katherine and Leia. "How was your night?" John boomed. "Did you brave the hotel, or did you chicken out?"

"Oh, and did you see the police cars out front this morning?" Trishelle chimed in. "Someone had a wild night. You didn't break the waiver, did you?"

"About that," Leia began, her leg bouncing double time.

"It was a memorable night." Katherine set her mug down. "We need to talk. Before you hear it from someone else."

John's jovial mood evaporated, replaced by the steely calm of a man accustomed to grim tidings. "What is it? Did they find Roger?"

"Yes," Katherine said simply. "He'd been dead for a while."

Leia nodded. "We found him in our room last night. Buried in the wall."

"Oh." Trishelle brought a hand to her mouth.

John recoiled. "That's insane. How did that happen?"

There was no easy way to say it. "Eric put him there."

Trishelle stared at her, then turned to John, who appeared equally stunned.

"Wait." He shook his head. "Eric? I don't understand."

Katherine chose her next words carefully. "Roger had been blackmailing Eric for years. That's how he kept winning."

"Four years in a row," Trishelle said, realization dawning.

"Eric was creating the plans Roger used to win every time," Katherine explained.

"Hold on." John stood, then sat back down. "Eric was losing to him on purpose?"

"That's impossible," Trishelle said. "Eric is a fighter. He can't even bring himself to lose a game of checkers against his five-year-old niece."

Katherine interlaced her fingers. "Eric confessed to us last night."

"Early this morning," Leia corrected.

"Right," Katherine said.

"After Katherine and I dug out Roger's hand in the wall next to our bed."

"You what?" John gaped.

Katherine took a deep breath. "Eric got into an altercation with Roger over the blackmail. It happened last Tuesday during the party. Eric attacked him." She folded her hands. "He concealed Roger's body in the wall that night before the hotel opened."

"It was the perfect hiding spot," Leia said. "It was convenient. Quick. No one would ever think to look—much less dare to go digging for it."

Katherine exchanged a look with Leia. He hadn't anticipated them. "He assumed he'd be long gone before the spring thaw revealed Roger."

John opened his mouth. Closed it. Opened it again. "And he admitted this to you?"

Katherine met his gaze. "He confessed everything."

Trishelle slipped her hand into John's. "I still don't understand why. What could Roger possibly have on Eric that would drive him to kill? Eric is a great guy. You don't know him like we do."

Katherine took a deep breath. "Eric killed Rebecca, and Roger knew."

"No." Trishelle shrank back. "No, he didn't. We were there. We witnessed her—" She forced herself to say it. "We saw her die."

The words hung heavy in the crisp morning air.

Katherine faltered, the weight of the moment bearing down on her. Leia's hand found her knee.

"Eric was having an affair," Leia began steadily. "Rebecca found out. They fought. Eric persuaded her to keep it between them until they could get marriage counseling, but he was just buying time. He knew she'd leave him, and he couldn't risk a messy divorce with his new restaurant opening, so he..." She paused, choosing her words carefully. "He sabotaged their ice sculpture. Told her where to stand for the filming and made sure it would fall on her when Craig made the final cut."

Trishelle gasped.

John swallowed hard. "Good heavens." He held his wife tighter. "We consoled him. We supported him and his dreams and his restaurant and everything."

"I felt sorry for him." Trishelle clutched her husband's leg, clinging to the closest part of him. "He's a monster."

John's mouth formed a grim line. "How can we catch him?"

"We need to let the police handle it," Trishelle insisted.

"No," John countered. "You and I both know he'll never admit this to the police."

Katherine reached for her cup of mocha. "The police apprehended him with the evidence in hand. He was fleeing the hotel. They have him in custody right now."

"They do?" Trishelle stared. "How?"

"Your picture roll tipped us off," Leia explained. "We

saw Roger's room design and realized he used it to start the rumor about Amy sleeping with the head judge. He'd carved the accusation in a picture code into the walls, knowing it would upset her. Once we determined Roger could manipulate someone like that, we figured the triangles meant something too."

Katherine nodded. "In our room, we found clues carved into the wall, suggesting Rebecca's death wasn't an accident. But it was odd—Roger had done an ancient Egyptian theme with no pyramids. It didn't add up. He'd been using the triangles to remind Eric that he knew how Eric had sabotaged his own sculpture. He wouldn't pass up the chance in an Egyptian room of all places. We figured that meant someone had erased them. That's when we decided to investigate further. So we dug a hole in the wall where the pyramids should have been, and we found Roger's body."

"We needed to know," Leia added. "For Rebecca. For you. For her family and everyone who loved her."

Trishelle swallowed hard, her eyes glistening. "All this time, it's been so difficult coming here. Rebecca's parents couldn't bring themselves to return at all. We thought the ice killed her, but..." She closed her eyes briefly. "He would have killed her no matter what. It wasn't the ice. It was him the whole time."

"Thank you both," John said, his voice thick. "You risked a lot to uncover the truth."

"It was the right thing to do," Leia said.

It was more than that, Katherine realized. She took Leia's hand and squeezed. "We've come to think of you as friends. And we'd go to the ends of the earth for our friends."

## CHAPTER
# TWENTY-FIVE

Katherine raised a glass of water with a cucumber floating in it. "I can't believe the resort's solution to us finding a body in the wall was to give us spa vouchers."

Leia fished the cucumber out of her own glass and tried it on one eye. "At least they didn't make us pay for the wall."

On the way up to the relaxation grotto, they'd stopped to watch Eric being led off the property in handcuffs. He'd confessed to Rebecca's murder. To killing Roger.

To everything.

Katherine didn't see where he'd had much of a choice, considering he'd gone through the trouble of assembling every bit of evidence against himself.

And it was damning.

"We did good," Leia said, giving up on the cucumber and taking a bite.

The door to the lobby cracked open. "I swear I just left my phone in here," Caitlyn said over her shoulder. She stopped when she realized she had company. "Katherine. Leia." Her face lit up. "I knew you'd be back for more."

"It's been a wild couple of days," Leia said in the understatement of the year.

Caitlyn's smile faltered. "I heard you found Roger in the wall." At Katherine's nod, she continued, "Thank you. Once it was certain he was gone, a few of his crew came forward to clear Amy's name. They're telling everyone how Roger lied and that Amy never swayed that judge."

Leia sat up straighter. "I'm so glad."

"Me too," Katherine was quick to say. It shouldn't have taken Roger's death for Larry and the others to speak up, but at least they'd found the courage now. "Amy deserves to be vindicated." And Katherine knew Roger's old team would thrive under Larry's leadership.

"That's not all," Caitlyn gushed, barely containing herself. "You missed a great ceremony. Amy's team won first place! I rounded them up for pictures, and then..." She scooped up her phone from a table near the door. "Check this out."

She displayed a photo of Carlos down on one knee before an elated Amy, the mermaid sculpture the perfect backdrop.

Katherine smiled warmly. "What a beautiful way to start their new life together."

"She deserves all the happiness in the world," Leia added.

"I'm not shocked he proposed." Caitlyn beamed. "But doing it here, in front of everyone? Carlos is smitten."

"As he should be." After all Amy had endured, she'd found someone who truly cherished her.

Caitlyn pocketed her phone. "The prize money is

## CHAPTER TWENTY-FIVE

enough for them to secure a space for their urban art studio. It'll be a fresh start for both of them. Carlos is already talking about youth programs and city-sponsored murals."

"I couldn't be happier for them," Katherine said, meaning every word. She'd misjudged Carlos, and now Amy had found a partner who genuinely cared. "Everyone deserves a second chance."

"I'd better go," Caitlyn said, patting her pocket. "Amy and Carlos should be done kissing by now."

"Lovely meeting you," Leia said.

"Congrats again," Katherine added.

Caitlyn playfully tapped a spa menu placard. "Try the Reindeer Milk and Honey Soak. I know it sounds wild, but it's pure bliss in a tub."

"Is there anything in here you haven't tried?" Leia joked.

"Actually, no. I like to treat the spa menu more like a cover-all bingo card, and I suggest you do the same. Have fun," she said before the door snicked closed behind her.

"The reindeer can keep their milk," Leia declared.

"I'd try it in ice cream," Katherine said.

They'd barely settled back down when the door opened again.

"Forget something else?" Leia asked.

But it was Trishelle who peeked in. "I heard you were in here."

"Are they dressed?" John asked from behind the wall.

"They're fine," Trishelle said, motioning him in.

"Come in," Katherine said. "I feel like we're holding court," she whispered to Leia.

"Does this mean I get a tiara?" Leia asked.

Knowing Leia, she was only half joking.

"We just wanted to say thank you again," Trishelle told them as John appeared behind her.

"We talked with Rebecca's parents," John added. "It meant so much to them to know what really happened. And to know that Eric will answer for what he did."

"Now that they know, they want to come back," Trishelle said, stepping fully into the room. "They want to join us for next year's event, to celebrate the competition and the art that Rebecca loved."

"I'm so glad," Leia said, rushing to give her a big hug.

Katherine stood as well. "It means so much that we could bring them peace."

"We had them on the phone when Amy won," John said, getting choked up. He cleared his throat. "Did you hear how everyone knows now that she never..." He gestured with his hand.

"We heard," Katherine said, saving him the discomfort.

"Rebecca would have been glad to see that, too. Her parents decided then and there to do more to encourage women to join the sport. They're putting together a scholarship in Rebecca's name to cover all expenses and fees for at least one more woman a year to compete for the first time."

"I love it," Leia exclaimed.

"And they'll be here to see their first scholarship winner take part," Katherine said.

"You can be here, too," Trishelle reminded them.

"Maybe," Leia said in a tone Katherine knew meant *I don't think so.*

"We may need a little time," Katherine said, backing her up. "But we did have an amazing weekend with you this year."

"We did too," Trishelle said, giving her a big, unasked-for hug.

"Thank you," John said, when Trishelle had pried herself away. "Thank you for standing up for Rebecca, for looking deeper when you realized something was wrong."

"How could we not?" Leia asked.

"You made a real difference," John said.

Leia's ears turned pink. "How kind of you to notice."

"How could we not?" John asked, stealing her line.

Was it possible to love these two more?

"You were right when we first met at the cabin," Katherine said. "This experience was better with new friends. I'm so glad we met." It was that simple.

"I was telling John last night how fun it's been getting to know you. But to know you were watching out for us? And for Rebecca as well? It's more than I could have imagined." She clasped her hands. "How lucky we were to run into you both."

Katherine felt the corner of her mouth twitch up. "From what I recall, you knocked on our door."

John laughed heartily.

"I did indeed." Trishelle beamed.

A scandalized spa attendant drew up behind John. "Sir! This is the ladies' relaxation grotto," she said as if he'd wandered into the pope's private confessional.

Katherine snickered. Then Leia. Then everybody else.

Well, except for the attendant.

The woman's jaw locked. "Please, sir!"

"You mean this isn't The Lumberjack's Lodge?" John asked innocently.

"We're going," Trishelle said, trying to keep a straight face but failing. "We'll be in touch," she promised before the attendant closed the door with the three of them firmly behind it.

"Our new friends are troublemakers," Katherine concluded, making her way back to her chair.

"The best kind," Leia agreed.

"Just like your bird."

"Hey, I bought her a fancy snowball ornament as a reward for saving my life."

"She'll tear it apart in a day."

"She'll make it snow stuffing all over the house." Leia grinned.

"And strut around like she's won the parrot Olympics while doing it." Katherine sank into the cushions. "This trip was completely crazy, but I don't regret one minute." For the first time in ages, she felt free. Alive. Ready to take on anything.

"Thanks for coming," Leia said, raising her water glass in a toast.

"Thanks for having a crazy idea." Katherine toasted her right back.

Leia took a sip. "You know, we could do it again," she said over the rim of her glass.

"What? Sleep in a room with a body in the wall? Chase down a killer?" Hardly. "I'm done roughing it, and I have the spa certificate to prove it."

"We can pick another adventure. An easier one this time."

Katherine lost her smirk.

"We have a whole lunchbox full of dreams and wishes," Leia reasoned, tempting her into following the white rabbit to Wonderland.

Or perhaps into opening Pandora's box.

The kicker was she kind of wanted to do it.

At least she wanted to be the kind of person who would do it.

"The lunchbox is back at the cabin," she said, trying the idea on.

"It's right here." Leia fished it from her massive spa bag.

Of course it was.

Ponies frolicked on the outside as Leia cracked it open. It was all happening so fast. "Come on. Let's go on another trip. This one will be more relaxing."

Innocent-looking paper hearts nestled inside. "How can you be sure?"

"It's got to be more relaxing than chasing down a killer in an ice hotel." She held out the box. "Why don't you do the honors this time?"

Why not?

Katherine reached inside and dug down to the very bottom. Her fingers caught on a folded heart in the far back corner. "This one," she said, opening it.

Leia bounded up from her lounger and perched next to her. "It's one of yours!"

"It is." She recognized her own neatly blocked letters.

*I wish we could have sailed on the Titanic.*

Katherine folded the paper back up. "Why did I say that? It sank."

And why was she taking advice from a ten-year-old? Even if it was her.

Leia swiped the heart and smoothed it out again. "Probably because it was such a beautiful ship, and no one really got to appreciate being on it."

"Yes, because it sank," Katherine repeated dryly.

Leia cocked her head. "You're very hung up on that."

Facts were facts. "It's hard to forget."

"Okay, well," Leia said, pondering. "I don't think we can get ourselves onto the actual *Titanic*—"

"I'm not that good a swimmer."

But Leia was all business. "I have an idea. Do you trust me?"

"I'll always trust you, but I also know when you're up to something." She had that look. It never changed.

"This time it will be a relaxing vacation," Leia vowed.

"On a doomed ship."

"On a *one-of-a-kind* ship," Leia gushed, growing more excited at the prospect.

This was going to be another stretch, just like the ice hotel.

"We did have a lot of fun on this trip." More than she'd ever imagined. "Promise me I won't regret this."

"You'll have an unforgettable adventure," Leia promised, closing the box.

Close enough. "To our next adventure," Katherine said, raising her cucumber water.

"May it be crazier than the last." Leia grabbed her glass and completed the toast. "Even if we never leave the dock."

"Don't say that," Katherine warned, only half joking. "This one was crazy enough."

"Oh, come on. To adventure!" Leia went for another toast.

"To adventure." Katherine clinked and took a hearty drink. "After all, what could possibly go wrong?"

# ACKNOWLEDGMENTS

A huge thank you to the amazing folks at Hôtel de Glace at Village Vacances Valcartier Resort in Quebec. Not only did you let two mystery writers wander around your stunning ice hotel (we promise we didn't break anything!), but you showed us the true meaning of Canadian hospitality. We're still in awe of what your artists create each winter—and yes, we solemnly swear we didn't hide any bodies in the ice walls.

To the wonderful people of Quebec City: merci beaucoup for welcoming us with open arms and endless recommendations for the best hot chocolate spots. We came for research and left with frozen noses, warm hearts, and enough inspiration to fill a dozen books. Our fictional ice hotel may be full of murder and mayhem, but the real Hôtel de Glace is pure magic.

**Don't miss the next Wanderlust mystery**
***Death on the Queen Mary***

***Best friends Kat and Leia are back…***
*This time they're boarding the Queen Mary for "A Night of a Thousand Stars"—a dazzling weekend gala to celebrate the historical ship's most glamourous voyage. But when an aging starlet threatens to expose what really happened during that fateful crossing, someone ends up dead.*

*What secret could be worth killing for after all these years? And how far will someone go to keep the Queen Mary's darkest secret buried at sea?*

# ABOUT THE AUTHORS

After decades of being each other's first readers and creative cheerleaders, Angie Fox and Kristin Bailey have decided to join forces and write the kind of adventures they'd want to go on themselves.

So far, they've survived an ice hotel (without digging into any walls), explored a possibly-haunted ocean liner (no comment on the ghost situation), and keep accidentally-on-purpose finding new places that "absolutely must" be researched in person.

The Wanderlust series is all about best friends who solve mysteries in bucket-list destinations. Thanks for coming along on this latest trip! We promise many adventures to come.

# ABOUT ANGIE FOX

*New York Times* and *USA Today* bestselling author Angie Fox now has photographic proof that a person really can get stuck on an ice slide. She prides herself in taking one for the team.

When she's not off on adventures, Angie writes sweet, fun, action-packed mysteries. Her characters are clever and fearless, but in real life, Angie is afraid of basements, bees, and going up stairs when it's dark behind her. Let's face it: Angie wouldn't last five minutes in one of her books.

Angie makes her home in St. Louis, Missouri with a football-addicted husband, two kids, and Moxie the dog. You can find Angie online at www.angiefox.com.

# About KC Bailey

Kristin has been writing critically acclaimed adventure-fantasy novels for young teens since 2013. With books described as "Tender and magical," now she has found her way home to her favorite genre since childhood, mystery.

When she is not figuring out how to kill people and not get away with it, she enjoys filling every spare cabinet with crafting supplies, learning languages, tending her large vegetable garden, birdwatching, pampering her mustang mare, and posting funny pictures of her cats online.

Printed in Great Britain
by Amazon